The CROWN of RUTHIN

Titles in this series

The Emerald Crown
Islands of the Inner Sea
Ghosts of Mehan'Gir
The Spoiled Land
The Ruby Hand
Voices of the Gods
The Dragon Sea
Mage Assassin
Daughter of the Guild
The Crown of Ruthin

DAUGHTER OF THE GUILD

First Print Edition, 2024

ISBN 978-1-909420-42-7

Cover Design by Diana Buidoso

Published by Asquith Publishing

The CROWN of RUTHIN

The Four Trophies, Book 10

L J Chappell

Asquith Publishing, Edinburgh

Contents

A Map of Central Mehan'Gir

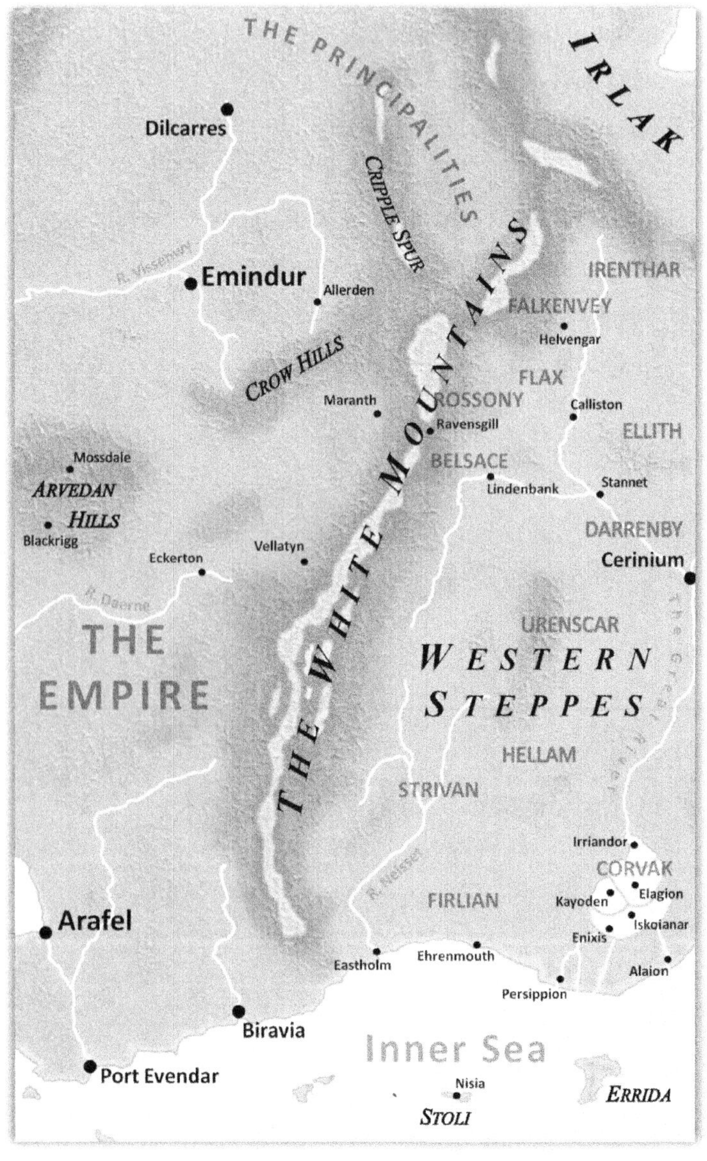

What Has Gone Before ...

In his guise as Kiergard Slorn, Prince Dalleric's plan to recover the Crystal Sword has been further delayed. Instead, he has risked returning to the Imperial Court to deliver a package to his cousin Rena, hoping to learn more from her about the murders carried out by the Human Lanvik and the assassin Foxblade. Moreover, Magda has not recovered from her injuries and his Company is being hunted by a Confederacy Death Squad.

Meanwhile, his own infatuation with Elisha of Giren Pass is at best unsettling and at worst a growing obsession.

Pireon may have returned to Elagion and his religious education, but he has been further distracted by a letter from his dead parents and by the announcement that his childhood crush will soon bond with his older brother Dach. His heart now lies with Iera, a student of the Oracle: he is currently facing the consequences of demonstrating his commitment to her.

Armed with fresh information concerning the murder of her family, Foxblade has left the Guild of Assassins, travelled deep into the Empire and executed her own mother. Her unexpected ally, General Aravan of the Aldarian Guard, has spent years building an army to retake her father's kingdom: now she must decide whether to join his venture and assume her birthright as Ruthin's rightful Queen.

Chapter One

Portents of War

1

The job seemed like the perfect antidote to so many weeks of inactivity: it was straightforward, paid reasonably well and involved very little risk.

Thawn preferred to listen from the end of the table while the rest of the Company discussed it. Although they always argued, often quite forcefully, she would be happy to go along with whatever they agreed. Her clanbrothers were with Kiergard Slorn, so she would have been concerned if there was to be much fighting, but their task was to retrieve a casket from a monastery and she didn't anticipate much requirement for trained swordarms.

'What's in the casket?' Vander asked.

'They don't say. It was donated a century ago by some local trader. Presumably a devotee.'

'And we're supposed to just steal it,' Ethryk checked. 'From a monastery?'

Bane turned over the papers he was reading. 'Apparently there was some dispute about whether it was his to donate in the first place, so perhaps we're returning it to its rightful owner. Does it bother you? Stealing from a monastery?'

'No.'

'Whose monastery is it?' Vrosko Din asked. 'What faith?'

'Brothers of Duraxi. About twenty monks.'

'They shouldn't offer much in the way of resistance. All they do is study the Book of Durac, which entails sitting around reading and arguing all day. So they're usually fat or old, often both.'

'Sounds perfect,' Lisamel smiled.

'Depending on how much we get paid …?' Tremano prompted.

'Two hundred and fifty.'

Two hundred and fifty Crowns seemed a lot for stealing from fat monks.

'Are the clients anticipating trouble?' Vorrigan asked, suspiciously.

'If they are, they don't say.'

'Then why haven't they got it themselves?'

'They might be a group of rival monks,' Lisamel suggested. 'Also fat and old.'

'Or perhaps they have moral scruples,' Menska said. 'About taking things from holy men.'

'Scruples which don't stop them employing someone else to do it …?' Bane disagreed. 'More likely, they don't want their involvement to be visible. Maybe they're local and prefer outsiders to do the job. We're to deliver the casket to an address in Vallierta, but the client might not be based there.'

There had never seemed a moment when they *weren't* going to take the job, but the deciding factor was that it was so local. The monastery sat on the slopes above the town of Fodetta on Comarenza, so there would be no long trips to the far side of Mehan'Gir. They would probably be back before Slorn.

'If we leave now, we can get there for Bellarna,' Ethryk pointed out. 'That'll be useful cover for strangers in town.'

The festival of Bellarna marked the end of winter, at the equinox, and was celebrated with loud processions and music that continued through the night.

Through winter, Cold Korridan, the God of the Dark and the Sea, had held sway but now six months of light would follow, presided over by High Belluhar, the God of the Air. Belluhar's influence over Wealth and Trade made the festival even more popular among the mercantile populations of the Inner Sea. The seasons had little direct effect on their business, but more distant markets and trade routes further north were sluggish during the colder months.

'Piastamo said he'd lay on something special for Bellarna,' Tremano said. 'He'll be disappointed.' Piastamo came in from the local village and cooked for them.

'It'll keep,' Bane said. 'Something to look forward to when we get back.'

'So do we leave now? Or in the morning?' Magda prompted, which ended the discussion. They had decided to take the job, it seemed, and the "we" indicated that Magda would be accompanying them.

'We can be there in time for the equinox either way,' Vander told them.

'Then we'll load up today and leave tomorrow morning,' Bane decided. 'There's no point sailing through the night if we don't need to.'

Hopefully being back out on the water would be good for Vander's state of mind. He was always happier at the helm of a boat: perhaps his mind was able to relax when it was occupied, or perhaps when it was occupied by nothing at all.

Over the last couple of months he had made efforts to move beyond his grief: he participated in conversations, sometimes joined in games, and he managed to stay more focussed on the people around him. More than that, he had finally moved out of the room he had shared with Aruel. He had kept her few possessions of course, but at least he had changed his surroundings.

Losing friends, comrades and loved ones was always difficult. Even when she was young, Thawn had learned about grief and the emotions that accompanied it: in Dog clan, the clan of fighters, loss was ever-present from the earliest age. There was no simple path through that grief, no method or training that would help. It would heal naturally in time without being forced, but that could take weeks, months or longer. Years later the sadness might still return for a moment, like an echo or a shadow, and there was nothing to do except let it wash over you.

She wondered if his efforts were the delayed result of a conversation he had with the assassin Foxblade, or the princess Vy'Rhienn, or whoever she was. Thawn had seen them talking late one night, aboard a stolen Confederacy launch on the way to Sivunder. He had talked about his time with Aruel, and Foxblade had told him quite directly to get on with his own life. That was nothing different than the others had already said, but perhaps it had helped that the assassin was young and beautiful and her eyes were silver. At that moment, Thawn would have sworn that there was something between them, some spark, but nothing had come of it so maybe she had been mistaken. The assassin had left now and there was no clear indication that they would ever meet again.

Vander's gradual transformation had helped lift the mood of the Company. No-one mentioned it, but what had happened to Magda had cast a dark shadow over them. She had always been at the heart of the group, irrepressibly cheerful like some carefree little sister, but now she was quiet and withdrawn, preoccupied. At times she seemed nervous and distracted, even fearful, and it almost felt as if the Company itself had been wounded.

The bruises were gone and many of the cuts and lacerations were only visible as rust-coloured lesions on her skin: some would vanish over time, no doubt, and others would become scars. She wore a metal and wood contraption around her damaged hands and fingers. Thawn had no idea if it actually helped: although Magda could hold things now, it was awkward and with very little strength.

Other than that, when she flexed her arms they looked slightly skew. And she still walked with a noticeable limp. According to Menska, they could break the bone in her leg again and try to set it straighter, but she advised waiting until a specialist could ensure the best result. And at some point, Thawn supposed she might address her missing teeth – she knew plenty people who used artificial teeth, or teeth from other Elves. Or she might choose to live with the spaces.

They prepared *The Thieving Priest* that afternoon and sailed after breakfast the next day.

Although their new ketch was far more comfortable than *Magda's Choice* had been, Thawn preferred the forced intimacy of the smaller boat. They had felt more like comrades in arms, which was how she sometimes thought of the others. She wasn't alone in preferring the older boat but she had avoided that discussion: there was no point – the change had been made.

The peaks of Comarenza appeared on the horizon three days later.

Typically for the Inner Sea, the interior was mountainous: forested and occasionally cultivated slopes descended in all directions to the more heavily populated coastal plain. The only significant event in the island's history had been six hundred years earlier, when twelve of the Inner Sea's merchant-princes fought a brief and ill-advised war against the Empire. A tactically brilliant but strategically suicidal victory against the Imperial fleet led to a backlash of economic and military annihilation, followed by a brutal and humiliating occupation.

The Empire had visited its revenge on each of the merchant-princes but Comarenza, situated so close to Port Evendar, had borne the swiftest and perhaps the harshest retribution. The events of that brief conflict still hung over the island like a shadow, as did the ongoing punishment imposed by the Empire – every four years, the population surrendered one of their number to the Imperial Court. And every twelfth year, whoever they had chosen as Tribute was sacrificed in Darkfall, in the far north, at the winter solstice.

Comarenza had never regained its status as one of the pre-eminent islands of the Inner Sea, neither among the merchant-princes nor in comparison with Carissola, which habitually avoided any military or political entanglements and prospered as a result.

The town of Fodetta lay on the eastern slopes of the island, eight or ten miles inland along a navigable river. Even so, they chose to dock in Doventi on the coast: the *Thieving Priest* was large enough that she would have attracted unwanted attention in such a small town. Given the strenuous nature of the likely terrain, it was obvious that Magda would remain aboard. Menska would stay with her.

The Company had no plans to spend the night in Fodetta: apart from the avoidable expense, a large group of strangers would be memorable wherever they found accommodation. So instead, they took a leisurely two hour walk uphill the next morning and spent the afternoon scouting out the sleepy town in small groups. The streets were decked with colourful flags and other decorations for the festival and the quiet daytime bustle was punctuated by the occasional sound of musicians practising for later.

Judging by these preparations, the evening's celebrations would be a significant occasion for the local community, if not the entire area. It seemed likely that a number of the monks might make the short trip into town. They would wait until the festivities started before visiting the monastery.

'We'll be able to hide in the crowds if anything goes wrong,' Thawn said.

'If the monks overpower us, you mean?' Vorrigan smiled.

'Well, that priest in Haadar was pretty scary,' Vander said. 'We don't want to come up against any like him.' Despite being little more than a boy, the priest Pireon had overpowered and disarmed Lanvik, tricked his way into their group and then stolen the Emerald Crown. The Company had honoured the episode by naming their new boat after him.

'He was from Corvak, and we shouldn't meet any of them,' Vrosko Din assured him. 'Corvak priests stay in Corvak. Normally. These are Brothers of Duraxi. Trust me, they're only going to be dangerous if they sit on us.'

A couple of hours before fifth watch, when the sun was low and the light was dim but not dark, they set off along the track with their weapons drawn. Coupled with the size of their group, that would hopefully intimidate the monks enough that they wouldn't cause any problems.

The monastery comprised a number of simple stone structures ringed by smaller and brightly-painted wooden outbuildings. Small fields and gardens spread out across the slopes in all directions.

As they approached, Bane said, 'I don't want to alarm anyone, but those fields don't look tended – not recently, at least.' He was right – the ground was covered by a carpet of young weeds.

'And there's a burst irrigation ditch on the right,' Ethryk added. 'Someone should have seen to that.'

They stopped walking.

'Those prayer banners should be pale green, for the third month,' Vrosko Din said: 'Pale blue is the colour of the second month.'

'Almost as if something has happened to the monks …,' Bane said.

'I don't like this,' Tremano said.

It was possible that the place had simply been abandoned of course, but Thawn took a couple of paces backwards and scanned the deep shadows around the buildings. She spotted a flicker of movement at the far corner of the courtyard – someone adjusting their position to get a better look at the Company. 'We're being watched,' she told the others. 'This is a trap, and we're in the open. We should turn round now.'

'Nice and slowly,' Bane agreed. 'Keep your weapons down.'

'And stick together,' Thawn ordered. Until they knew the numbers against them, presenting the most formidable target was their best defence. Splitting up would make it impossible for their enemies to intercept them all, of course, but would also make it much more likely that some of them would be lost. They had to assume the worst, that they were the intended target and that their enemy was numerous, well-armed, trained and ruthless. On that basis, there would be at least one of them between the monastery and the town, and perhaps others closing from the fields around.

The Company couldn't risk a fight, not this group: Bane was formidable, but the others were no more than skilled amateurs. Garran and Tyrell were in the north with Kiergard Slorn.

As they retreated, she warned: 'They won't let us just walk away. Get ready to run.'

A few seconds later, perhaps on some signal that she missed, a number of figures emerged from inside or behind the monastery buildings. Out the corner of her eye, she spotted someone approaching from the fields on the left. She noted the way they moved, how they held their weapons, how they marked each others' positions and how they moved as a team. They were all Madarinn and they were all trained: they were familiar with each other, and they were executing a plan that had been agreed earlier.

As she had anticipated, someone was approaching from below. He seemed to be alone, but engaging him would slow the Company down and increase the overall risk.

She'd also noticed that a number of their unknown enemies were carrying bows.

'Off the road,' she ordered, pointing to the light forest on the right. 'The trees are your cover; remember to dodge. Get back to the town!'

They had practised this at Davata Lodge so they all knew not to move in straight predictable lines, and they were all fit enough to run. Still, her main concern was to protect the non-fighters and in the dimming evening light, there was a real danger one of them would trip. It was just as well they'd left Magda back at the boat – her condition was much better than three months ago, but she still couldn't have run any distance or with any agility.

Their pursuers might be faster and better trained, but Vorrigan and Lisamel had bows and a couple of volleys, however ineffective, made their enemies hesitate enough that the Company were able to maintain their lead. Before long, they could hear the sound of drums from the town ahead.

'Head for the parade,' Bane shouted.

And hope they don't have friends waiting for us.

The outlying sprawl of single-storey white houses was deserted, and they ran unobserved down the twisting cobbled alleys of sharp drops and uneven steps, weaving their way towards the noise. Eventually, they reached a throng of loud and enthusiastic revellers: judging by the numbers, people had flooded into Fodetta from the surrounding area. If they'd brought costumes, they could have easily vanished among the random chaos of the parade, but they hadn't prepared an escape plan.

Thawn was painfully aware that their group was too large and unwieldy to go unnoticed for long: even amongst all these people, the plainly-dressed Company would be easily spotted. The size of the group was also their biggest asset if it came to a fight, so she was reluctant to split them up.

'We need to get off the streets,' Bane echoed her thought.

Any of the buildings around them could be effectively defended, but would leave them effectively trapped. Of course, here in the centre of town the water gave them a different option.

She pointed and Bane nodded. 'River!' he shouted to the others.

They squeezed through the packed streets where the

festival was at its very loudest and emerged at the riverbank. A couple of wooden jetties jutted out into the water and Bane ran along the largest, almost to the end, and then bent down and swung himself over the side. The others followed him. Here, about a third of the way out into the current, the water was still barely more than chest deep. Ducking down, they pulled themselves underneath the walkway, where there was enough space for their heads to remain above the water. Thawn adjusted her position so that she was kneeling, uncomfortable and awkward: Bane must have found it much more difficult, being so much taller than the others.

And then they waited, holding on to the wooden struts and to each other, trying to squint through the gaps between the planks.

Eventually three of their Madarinn pursuers emerged on the shore. They walked back and fore, weapons drawn, scanning the little boats pulled up on the shore, until a fourth joined them briefly. After exchanging a few words they moved away in different directions.

'We need to get away from here,' Vorrigan said quietly, above the murmur of the water around them.

'They'll probably have people on the roads by now,' Bane warned. There were only three routes out of Fodetta, which would be easy to cover.

'What about the boats?' Tremano suggested. A number of shallow riverboats were tied up at the jetty, and others were lying on the stony shore.

'We'd need a couple, and we'd be an easy target if they spotted us,' Bane disagreed. 'We should wade across to the other bank.'

'I suppose we're already soaked,' Tremano said.

'Should we wait until it's darker?' Ethryk asked.

'The longer we wait, the more organised they'll get, and the more likely we'll have to fight.'

It wasn't ideal – they would be visible to anyone watching this particular stretch of the river – but Thawn couldn't think of a better plan. Right now, their pursuers would most likely be covering all the possible exits from Fodetta. Hopefully it would be a few minutes before they returned to the river.

Thank the Gods Magda isn't with us.

Half-wading and half swimming, the eight of them made their way directly across the river from the jetty. The current was faster at the centre and most of them lost their footing a couple of times, but they were fit and strong. Thawn was more concerned about them being seen: if their bobbing heads were spotted, there would be nothing they could do to get out the way of arrows or crossbow bolts.

Though it felt longer, it took hardly more than a minute before they were pulling themselves out of the water on the far bank. They crawled away from the shore and lay in the long grass looking back across the river for any sign that their departure had been observed. There was nothing, so they set off on foot for the coast.

As well as contending with the darkness, their clothes were wet and heavy and they chose to avoid the string of tiny settlements along the river, so their walk took longer than they had hoped. When they finally reached the river mouth, they paid a boatman to carry them east, back to Doventi. There were Bellarna celebrations in the streets there as well, more extravagant and better organised than in Fodetta and with far more people both watching and participating.

Their enemies might have people here as well, so they moved quickly and cautiously back to the boat. They found Menska and Magda sitting on deck waiting for fireworks or some procession to the water's edge, as often happened in coastal towns during festivals.

'We need to cast off, now,' Vrosko Din said, as Thawn shepherded the others onboard and then stood on deck, scanning the harbour's edge for any sign of danger. Bane was already untying the ropes that held *The Thieving Priest,* and Vander had taken the wheel; Lisamel and Vrosko Din worked the sails. It was only a few seconds before the light breeze caught the mizzen and they pulled gradually away from the harbour wall. The others hauled the mainsail halfway up, and their boat glided effortlessly between the harbour walls and out into the Inner Sea.

'Well?' Magda asked. She had stayed on deck.

'It was a trap. There haven't been monks there for weeks.'

'A trap for us?'

'We have to assume so,' Bane said.

'They were all Madarinn,' Thawn added. 'Trained.' There was no avoiding the implication that they were Confederacy, presumably the Death Squad that had been hunting them since Slorn's raid on An'Holt and theft of the Ruby Crown.

They sailed through the night rather than anchoring offshore.

'Even if they're still looking for *Magda's Choice*, they're professionals,' Magda said, as they sat below. 'They'll take their time checking the harbour records across Comarenza, starting in Edrillo.' Edrillo was the largest town, on the west coast.

'They'll be thorough,' Ethryk agreed.

'And after they're done, *The Thieving Priest* might not be at the very top of their list, but she's going to be pretty close,' Magda continued. 'She docked close to Fodetta, she's the right size for the Company and she only stayed a day.'

'Kiergard Slorn is not going to be happy when he hears about this,' Bane said, grimly.

2

Pireon's extra duties lasted for well over a month after he ran naked through the Refectory, and only then did his classes with Ykerios start again. For days, he rehearsed what he would say to the Hierarch – most versions were apologetic, many were contrite, a few were frivolous – but the subject of his transgression didn't arise.

At least, not directly.

Instead, Ykerios inquired how Pireon's relationship with Iera was "settling down", which at least demonstrated that he had now gone to the trouble of committing her name to memory.

Over the following week or two, it became clear that Pireon was struggling to concentrate or to focus.

'It seems that you're even less use when you're happy than when you're miserable,' the Hierarch observed.

But it was more than that. Since returning from his pursuit of the Emerald Crown, Pireon had found it difficult to adjust to life on Elagion. He felt an uneasy restlessness, like a permanent itch: not necessarily for physical travel – the idea of spending any more nights away from his own bed sometimes made him shudder. But rather, he felt stifled by the limited opportunities available to him each day: by not being in control and not making his own decisions.

In their seventh class, the Hierarch chose to discuss a passage from *The Eastern Laments*. Rahkon had come ashore near Shamura; Dimir had joined them, bringing death with him.

'It's easy to skim over those words – "bringing death with him" – but what does it actually mean?' Ykerios asked. 'What death? Does the author mean Rahkon's death – is he somehow blaming Dimir, even though Dimir isn't involved in the argument. It's a puzzle, but one that we can solve …'

Pireon forced himself to focus: 'We could look at what else happens in the text: whether anyone else blames Dimir or his presence for what happens to Rahkon. Or we could look at other places where the author uses the same language to describe Dimir, and where it's clearer what the meaning is.'

'Reasonable,' the Hierarch noted, 'but not actually useful.'

Pireon nodded: he was familiar with the rest of the *Laments*, and there were no such references. 'If there was another text that referred to the same incident, then that might shed light on the meaning here.'

'Yes. Good. But, again, we know that Rahkon's death isn't referred to in any of the other scriptures.'

'We could go back to the original text,' Pireon suggested, after a pause.

'Let's do that, then,' the Hierarch agreed. 'After all, errors and ambiguity can creep into any translation, no matter how careful the work and how skilful the translator.'

For centuries almost all study of Scripture used translations created here on Elagion. Before that, people had needed to learn the ancient languages just to read their own holy books but now everything was available to everyone, in a language so common there wasn't even a name for it. But no translation ever meant exactly the same as the original, and some meanings or subtleties could easily have been lost by the translators, no matter how careful they had been. Pireon had been taught that in his very first Ancient Languages lesson as a Novice.

'And that's why we study the original languages,' the Hierarch continued. 'There's no point being able to go back to the original texts if we can't read and understand them.'

He pushed himself up from his chair and walked across to a wall of bookshelves. 'I keep copies of all the books of scripture here, and a lot of other interesting volumes. They should really be in the Library – or the Archive, most of them – but that's one of the privileges of being Hierarch: they let me keep whichever books I fancy. Actually, there is no "they",' he chuckled. 'I just take the books and nobody dares object.'

He returned carefully to his armchair – he had managed the short walk without relying on his staff, but he had held onto the back of the chair, the edge of the table and the bookcase itself as he moved across the room.

'So, which canon does *The Eastern Laments* belong to?'

'The Terevarna,' Pireon said. Scripture was almost evenly split between the Terevarna and the Madarinn language.

'Of course it is. But just consider for a moment how strange it is that millennia ago Dark Elves and Light Elves read different books of Scripture even though they believed in the same Gods.' He paused, with a glint in his eye. 'Now, if there are Four Races – as is popularly believed – then why are the other two Races so poorly served with holy books?'

'Perhaps the Dragon Lords have holy books,' Pireon speculated. 'How would we know?'

'Oh, very good,' Ykerios smiled. 'Yes, they might. Wouldn't that be a thing! Whole books of Scripture that we know nothing about? Fresh tales of the Twelve Gods and their teachings. What a wonderful idea, that the Dragon Lords worship the same Pantheon as us through different texts. But what about the Humans? We know they don't have books like these, and not so many of them believe in the Twelve Gods …'

Pireon didn't answer and the Hierarch simply smiled: they were just playing with ideas. He laid the copy of the *Laments* on the table and turned over the pages until he reached the seventeenth chapter. 'Here,' he said. 'Here comes Dimir … *estrtsa kmih hirr trch'ta*.'

'Ah,' Pireon nodded.

'Ah?'

'The translators might have been better to use "bearing" or "carrying" rather than "bringing",' Pireon said. In the original, there was no suggestion of any metaphorical meaning. 'The implication is that wherever Dimir goes, death is part of him. Like his possessions or his clothes.'

'Good,' Ykerios nodded.

'Should we change it, Father?'

'What do you mean?'

'Should we change *The Eastern Laments* to make the meaning clearer? Even if most copies are produced elsewhere, the original translations were made on Elagion so we should be able to make corrections and changes. I'm sure everyone else would follow our lead.'

Ykerios started laughing. 'What a fantastic and outlandish idea,' he exclaimed. 'Far from everyone else following our lead, that would most likely create a great religious divide between followers of the old and new versions. There are many people who think that the words in this translated version are holy and perfect. To them, any suggestion we might alter them would be heresy. And plenty others would believe that we were changing the religious texts for secret and pernicious reasons of our own. But still … what a wonderful notion.'

When he finally stopped chuckling, the Hierarch took the discussion in a different direction by asking: 'This common language that we all speak now – where did it come from?'

'I don't know,' Pireon admitted. It hadn't been discussed in any of his classes.

'No-one does, really, but you must have some ideas. Is it a version of one of the ancient languages?'

'Em, no. No. It's nothing like either of them. Even the words that the other languages have in common are completely different from the words we use today. So maybe …'

'Yes?'

'Perhaps we're speaking a version of the Human language. Or the Dragon Lord language.'

'Perhaps we are. Many scholars believe it's the language

of the Humans but we can't be certain. There are no Human writings as old as Scripture, so we simply don't know what language they used to speak. There's another theory that there was a fifth language, a trading language that all Four Races used, and our common tongue developed out of that. Some people believe that both theories are true – that the Human language *was* the language everyone used for trading …'

'But if there were five different languages, how in the Three Lands did people talk to each other?'

'With difficulty, I imagine. We have stories of wars starting by accident because of people not understanding each other. Even now, people use different words to describe the same thing …'

'Yes.' Pireon could think of a dozen examples, most of which he'd learned during his recent trip.

For the last few minutes of the lesson, they discussed the advantages and disadvantages of everyone speaking the same language and then, before Pireon left, Ykerios remarked, 'I understand your family has set a date for Dachaeron's bonding.'

'Yes. Dach told me.' His brother had received a letter from their Uncle Quiron that morning.

'They haven't asked me to officiate,' the Hierarch continued. 'Sometimes the Great Families do that, but perhaps I'm out of favour with the Kiritas. Maybe said something controversial …'

'I haven't heard anything like that.'

'Well, you wouldn't have. Maybe I should just turn up and put the fear of the Twelve Gods in them. I haven't been to Kayoden in years.'

'I'm sure you'd be welcome,' Pireon said. 'I can suggest it, if you like.'

'Thank you, but no,' the Hierarch shook his head. 'The journey would be far too much effort … though it does make me think that I've been shut away on Elagion for too long. I should make some official progression around the Floating Cities again. Remind them all what I look like. Remind them that I haven't died.'

Despite what he said, the Hierarch in fact travelled regularly around the Floating Cities – not only to perform investitures and sacraments, but to attend meetings of the two Councils that ruled Corvak together with the Priesthood. This year, though, he seemed to have left Elagion less frequently than Pireon remembered.

'Mind you,' Ykerios was still musing, 'a grand trip like that seems like an awful bother. So maybe I won't. And there's no way I can manage Darkfall again: not there and back. Someone else is going to have to do that for me … after all, they don't even have the Crown any more.'

Their meeting ended on that slightly unexpected note.

The rest of Pireon's afternoon comprised three classes – Ancient Languages, appropriately, followed by Relics and a double lesson in Devotions. After the evening meal he had three hours of duties to perform, and only then would he be able to spend any time with Iera.

Although it was accepted that relationships occurred on Elagion, no concessions to the daily calendars were made to accommodate them. If Iera had been studying for the Orders, then there would have been a dozen moments through each day when they could have met briefly: they could have eaten meals together and perhaps arranged to share some of the duty rotas, as Dach and Ajiila sometimes managed.

Pireon couldn't help envying his brother's situation.

Even their current arrangement, when they both slept in dormitories and had no private personal space without the assistance and goodwill of their friends, was significantly better than Pireon could hope for with Iera. The Seminary maintained an accommodation block specifically for bonded couples: he assumed Dach and Ajiila would have a room arranged already, or at least be on the waiting list. So in the future they would have a place with their own door.

In contrast, the Oracle complex was at the northern tip of Elagion and even though its Students shared the same Refectory building as the Seminary, they ate at different times.

Within the strictures of the weekly timetable, Pireon and Iera could normally rely on a few pre-planned minutes together at the Library, the only other facility that was shared. Beyond that, they had a brief window each evening which they normally spent at the Oracle Sanctuary: Iera's private room afforded them much more privacy than the Seminary and from a practical standpoint he walked much faster than she did. Even so, he resented his daily fifteen minute walk for eating into their limited time together.

Worse, since his public transgression in the Refectory the older priests seemed to pay particular attention to his observance of night-time curfew, as well as his general behaviour. They individually checked his presence at lights out, which he never remembered them doing previously, so he had no leeway to explore alternative arrangements. Even setting aside the curfew rules, the beds in the Oracle complex were awkwardly narrow and didn't look as if they would support the weight of two people, even if one of them was as light as Iera. And the one chair in her room felt as if it had been deliberately designed to be uncomfortable.

There was no-one he could even commiserate with. As far as he knew, they were the only couple sustaining a relationship between the Seminary and the Oracle: if another existed, then they were concealing it.

He hadn't asked Iera, but there didn't seem to be any relationships at all within the Oracle, though a number of her colleagues seemed conspicuously affectionate with each other. Unlike the Seminary, they had no accommodation for bonded couples. There *were* no bonded couples. How could there be, when any Adept might be called by the Oracle to a lifetime of service?

He didn't like to dwell on the thought, but this might be as close as his relationship with Iera would ever be. Living apart, never to be bonded and always second to the Oracle.

There were rumours of exotic carnal rituals associated with the Psirogant and the Oracle, which inevitably fed the colourful imaginations of the other boys in his dormitory. He had no idea how they found out, but they knew about his relationship almost immediately and seemed to feel that it was their duty and their right to comment on it at length.

At least at first.

But they sometimes met Iera at the Refectory and she made a point of talking with them individually, however briefly. She knew their names and a little about each of them, and those casual contacts seemed to reduce the level of teasing below what he would have expected. Of course, that might also have been because her infirmities still made them uncomfortable. Awkward. None of them mentioned anything, but around her they were louder and their casualness seemed forced.

They also resisted the coarser goading about the physical side of his relationship that other neophytes received: those who were seeing girls from the Orders. Not that there *was* any physical side to their relationship. Not in that sense.

When he at last reached her room, they stood and hugged, basking in the thrill of physical contact and the joy of being together. Everything he did with her, even simply holding her hand and entwining his fingers in hers, felt fresh and intimate: something that would never become stale or routine.

They could have spent forever in that embrace, but stepped apart when each felt that the other might be uncomfortable. And, of course, they had less than half an hour before he would have to leave again.

There was no plan to these brief meetings, but every evening became a memory to treasure because it had been with her, whether it was a conversation, a quiet moment admiring a view or simply sharing a snack. This evening they talked and he told her about the date for Dach's bonding, a couple of weeks after the equinox.

'You should come,' he suggested. 'To Kayoden.'

'I can't. Not really,' she disagreed.

That could have meant a lot of things. She might not feel physically capable of the journey, or perhaps she wanted to avoid the pressures of the social occasion. She might not find the idea appealing, or might have more important things to do on Elagion. Perhaps she wanted to avoid meeting his family, at least on the premise that they were a couple. Or perhaps she was already such a part of the Oracle that she felt uncomfortable leaving Elagion at all: unlike Senior Priests, who were normally despatched to postings all across Corvak after their training, Voices and Speakers remained in the Oracle complex. People came to the Psirogant to receive her words: she did not go to them.

'It wouldn't be a problem,' he assured her.

'Alright,' she smiled. 'I'll think about it.'

'Gods, you are so bad at lying. Even when it's to make other people feel better.'

'I've never seen the point,' she admitted. 'And lying goes against everything they teach us: any form of deliberate deceit. On which subject …'

'Yes?' he asked, cautiously, wondering what particular "deceit" she was about to question him over.

'I was reading your letters again, … and you mentioned a Dark Elf called Vander. He came from somewhere in the Inner Sea and was good with boats.'

'Uh, Vander. Yes,' he confirmed, knowing exactly what she was about to say.

'Might this have been the same Vander who somehow escaped from Darkfall? The official Tribute from Arrento?'

'Yes,' he admitted. 'I think it probably was.'

'The one everyone's talking about? The one who was going to be executed, but now looks as if he might start a war?'

'Yes,' he repeated. He didn't know what else she wanted him to say.

'Why didn't you tell me?'

'I didn't know at the time. And when I found out, I thought it was probably a secret.'

'Even from me?'

'Even from you.'

'I think you're wrong. You have to tell me all your secrets now that we're a couple. Especially the interesting ones.'

'And you'll tell me all of yours?'

'I don't have any secrets.'

'I don't believe that for one second. Half of what you study at the Oracle is secret.'

'Secret, but extremely boring: nothing you would be interested in. If I tried to tell you, you might never speak to me again …'

It seemed like no time at all before he had to leave. She walked with him to the edge of the Oracle compound: their parting embrace in the shadows was always precious and fragile, knowing that it had to end before either of them was ready.

He smiled all the way south to the Circle and the Seminary beyond, his mood lifted by the time they had spent together and already anticipating tomorrow's fleeting visit. And the equinox was approaching of course, when their classes were suspended for a few days and they would be able to spend more time together.

If only she would change her mind and come to Kayoden with him … away from Elagion with its classes, duties, sacraments and rituals. He doubted he could persuade her, though, and part of him wasn't even sure he should try: after all, she'd already told him that she didn't want to come.

Before that trip, of course, there was the matter of Dach's graduation to Priest-Assistant.

Despite his hopes for an earlier date, the ceremony eventually took place on the equinox itself, immediately after the annual sacrament to High Belluhar. Almost one hundred priests were to receive new colours – more than Pireon remembered at any previous graduation. Including his brother, there would be five graduating to Priest-Assistant. Although he hadn't said anything, Dach would surely be frustrated at having to share the attention. Then again, he would have a huge audience: almost the entire Priesthood and Seminary would be present. If he knew his brother at all, then that would at least partly make up for having to share the occasion.

High Belluhar's sacrament would be performed at Temples across the Steppes and the Empire – everywhere the Pantheon was worshipped and the teachings of Corvak held sway – but Pireon doubted anywhere saw such large numbers as the Mother Temple. There were only be a few hundred in attendance from beyond Elagion, rather than huge numbers of pilgrims and the faithful that attended at other times in the calendar. And there was no-one there from the Oracle: the equinox was a holy time for them as well – the moment of perfect balance between light and dark, with light on the rise. In divine rapture, deep within the Sanctuary, the Psirogant would be granted a fresh Prophecy before the new dawn. But almost the entire Priesthood on Elagion *would* be present, together with the Orders: surely more than two and a half thousand souls.

As the last Novices took their places, the Temple felt almost full, even though it was built for many more.

A hush fell as the Hierarch entered in his white and gold robe, flanked by the twenty-four Senior Priests who would be performing the duties normally assigned to

Neophyte Priests or Initiates. Pireon breathed in deeply as the procession passed by: as well as the usual incense, the air was suffused with fragrant oils that filled his head and lined his throat. The walls danced with the flickering light of countless candles and although the Temple was dedicated to the Dead God, the icons from the chapels of Cold Korridan and High Belluhar had been arranged around the high altar.

The words of the sacrament echoed around the dome, each part spoken in unison by a chorus of voices, and Pireon could almost feel the weight of the centuries. These same words repeated every year in this same place, echoing down through time, were like a thread or a wick in a candle – something that had remained as solid and unchanging as any mountain.

He imagined generations of past Neophytes standing where he stood now, at this exact spot – on this very flag-stone. What had been happening across the Three Lands when they recited these words at this time and on this day? What were their concerns when Shamura was at its height? Or even earlier, during the war with the mages? Through it all, Elagion had remained constant and unchanging. The sacraments, festivals and other events in the calendar of Mother Church were like the ticking of an immense clock, marking the millennia.

When the ceremony was finished, the atmosphere in the Temple became palpably lighter as if everyone had exhaled and relaxed a little. From every direction, he heard the tiny noises of people clearing their throats and shuffling their feet as they stretched or changed position. The oils were still heavy in the air, but the last echoes of the holy words faded and left an almost palpable quiet behind them – a quiet broken by the rustling of thousands of people waiting to celebrate the promotions, elevations and graduations of their fellows.

Those progressing from Initiate to Priest-Acolyte

accounted for the majority: their appointments were made first and involved very little ritual. Pireon had shared classes with a number of them but there was no-one from his dorm, so there would be an even greater gap between him and the others. His own promotion had been premature, of course: he was still studying some material appropriate for Initiates and that might continue into the coming teaching session if his mastery of it wasn't deemed sufficient.

Graduations to Priest-Assistant, which included his brother, followed immediately after.

At twenty, Dach was by far the youngest, as well as the best known and most popular. Certainly, the whole assembly seemed to become slightly quieter when the Hierarch reached him, as if they were suddenly paying more attention, though the words and the ritual were no different from the other four. Despite everything that had happened to Pireon, he would no doubt be "Dach's brother" for at least another few years.

Following Dach's group, a number of Priest-Assistants became Priests-Nominate and then a further twelve were elevated to the black of Junior Priest. Finally eight Junior Priests were anointed. The graduation ceremony lasted almost as long as the sacrament, but after that the whole Priesthood spilled out into the afternoon sunshine in a buzz of excited voices and loud conversation.

There would be secondary sacraments and a schedule of additional duties throughout the following two days, but regular classes were suspended over the equinox. Frustratingly, the Oracle's schedule was not so relaxed. The Psirogant would issue a divine Prophecy and the ritual surrounding that would continue late into the night: from the lowliest Student to the Speakers, everyone at the Oracle would be in the Sanctuary. He spent most of the afternoon and evening with his friends, but still walked up to the Circle as the sun sank behind Lake Phyroneia and climbed the little hill. From the top he had a clear view north to the

Oracle, not that there was much to see – a handful of lights, and a few dark buildings: the Sanctuary was mostly underground, deep underground. Even so, he sat there for over an hour, feeling some small reward just from being a little closer to Iera.

The next morning, the dormitory was awakened at the usual hour. There might only be a handful of short services but the more mundane activities of the Seminary continued uninterrupted, so everyone had assigned duties to perform.

After breakfast, he visited the Library in case the Oracle had released anything of the previous night's revelations. At some point, extracts of her new Prophecies would be posted in major Temples and public buildings across Corvak and beyond: in some places, they were read aloud. But before that they were seen here on Elagion, not at the Mother Temple but at the Library.

The Speakers would continue studying the Psirogant's words, of course, and longer texts would be made available later. Parts of the Prophecy might only become clear when they were considered in the light of previous revelations, sometimes from years earlier. Since everything the Psirogant said was part of a larger truth, the Speakers looked for patterns and connections and the repetition of themes and phrases, to better understand where each piece fitted and to better comprehend the divine message.

The ritual would have lasted through much of the night and Iera had asked him not to come early: she would need to sleep.

The Prophecies were eventually posted an hour before lunch, and Pireon briefly joined the little huddle pushing to read them. They said nothing that he wouldn't have expected. Eventually, almost an hour after midday, he decided to head north on the main path to the Oracle buildings. He hadn't even reached the Circle when he encountered a group of Oracle Students walking in the opposite direction. Iera was with them.

She waved her friends to go on without her and told Pireon, 'I just woke up. I was coming down for some breakfast. Or lunch. And to see you.'

'We can go together,' he beamed, and they walked slowly back the way he had come, hand in hand. 'I've got a couple of small services this afternoon, and duties before and after the evening meal. But that's all. What about you?'

'Almost nothing,' she smiled. 'Two duties in the evening. A lot of the girls aren't even up yet. How was the sacrament?'

'It was good. Solemn. But uplifting.'

'And how's Dach? Priest-Assistant Dachaeron of Kiritas?'

'Oh, you know: insufferable.' He had talked to his brother briefly after yesterday's ceremony, as well as earlier that morning. 'How was the Oracle?'

'Haven't they posted anything yet?'

'Well yes.' That wasn't really what he'd been asking, but he summarised: 'The Dead God will be renewed this year: a new beginning to an old life and an old destiny. And there's a war coming.'

'There was a lot more than that,' she told him. 'The Speakers are still going through it.'

'Yes, but they're not going to come up with anything surprising, are they,' he shrugged.

'What's that supposed to mean?' she asked, sharply.

'You know. Most of what the Oracle posts isn't exactly clear, and it usually says things that are either really obvious or else so vague that they could mean anything.' He was echoing opinions that he'd heard from other people, but it felt increasingly awkward saying them to Iera.

'Are you not even worried that there's a war coming?' she looked exasperated.

'There's always a war coming,' he tried to make a joke of it: 'if you wait long enough.'

'Don't be flippant,' Iera scolded. 'The Psirogant doesn't mean "coming" in the future. She means coming *here*, to

Corvak. The Speakers left the word ambiguous, but it was clear from the way she said it.'

'Mm.' Pireon made a noise, reluctant to say more or to ask for details. He knew better than to argue about Prophecy with a Student of the Oracle.

3

Atterlie held the little enamel ring that her mother had given her in the palm of her right hand. It was more than fifteen years old now and covered in a lattice of tiny cracks but its colours were still bright. She hadn't worn it since she left Ruthin at the age of eight and now, every time she looked at it, she couldn't stop herself from remembering her mother's betrayal; the night her family had been murdered; the night she had abandoned her own brother Mironyx to the Imperial soldiers.

Miko.

The Guild had taught her not to succumb to her emotions: "passion chooses quickly, not wisely," they said. So she had kept the ring, threaded on a thin cord.

It might remind her of the night Ruthin fell but it also brought back memories of her mother in earlier times – she knew now that their relationship had never been entirely what it seemed but she had treasured the gift at the time and it was still precious to her. Regardless of how tainted it might have become, her bond with her mother helped define the person she became. So the ring had become a symbol as well as a memento of times that she could never recapture. But even if that life was gone forever, it would shape the new future that she would create, if she could, both for herself and for Ruthin.

She lifted the cord back over her head and let the ring drop under her tunic to lie unseen against her chest. Then she stepped out of the wooden hut that Aravan had assigned her, one of a row of twenty or thirty close to the centre of his community. The main barracks lay further out.

The General had created a whole town here, and more: tended fields stretched away beyond the clutch of buildings, but there was no mistaking the place for anything other than a military facility. Every hour of daylight was filled with soldiers training and drilling: permanent activity that kept them too busy to be bored or disaffected; kept them distracted from the simple reality that they had no homes, no families and none of the little freedoms and choices that made up an ordinary life.

For all of their dedication and training, the troops were old – not one of them under thirty – and most of them were slow. Few had seen any real action for years and that had dulled their reactions. Still, to have an army of any sort placed her in a better place than she could have imagined just three months earlier.

Of course, whatever General Aravan might say, they were *his* army. Not hers.

After she had settled matters with her mother, she fulfilled her promise to him by journeying south and sending him a message. Port Evendar was one of the larger cities of the Empire, at least three hundred thousand souls she supposed, but she became quickly bored of it while she awaited his response.

After almost four weeks, he came in person.

She found him waiting in the lounge of her hotel, sitting rigidly and economically in a small armchair with a glass and an open bottle of wine on the table in front of him. He stood, slightly awkwardly, when she walked over.

'You've been waiting long?' she asked, as they sat.

'Three hours, my lady. More or less.'

'Sorry. I was walking around the city. Again.'

'They told me at the desk. That you go out most days.'

'It's less tedious than sitting in my room.'

'Have you found nothing interesting to do, then?'

'Nothing.' She spent much of her time playing cards and dice and occasionally Fugitive, but most of the competent players were only interested in playing for money.

'Your personal business?'

'Concluded,' she nodded. That wasn't a subject she wanted to discuss in any detail.

'And the money?'

'Secure.' The considerable fee she had received for her last contract with the Guild of Assassins was sitting in a vault beneath the Imperial Treasury in Arafel, and it would remain there until she needed it. She had no intention of simply donating it to the General's war coffers. At least, not yet.

'So will you turn your attention to your duty now?'

'I will join your enterprise,' she confirmed, choosing not to rise to his jibe.

'That's excellent news,' he smiled. 'If you are with us, we are twice as likely to succeed. Will you share a drink with me?'

'One,' she nodded, 'and then I'll pack my bag. I have no wish to stay here any longer than I already have.'

They sailed south aboard the General's frigate *Night Princess*, to one of the tiny islands that lay east of Arrento.

'I thought about finding a haven in the Chain,' he explained, as the crew shortened the sails for their approach. 'It's an obvious place to hide, but there's far too much competition. And here is more convenient.'

'Richer pickings?'

'Not the way you mean, no. But here we are close to the Free Ports and their slave markets.' Aravan had recruited his men, veterans of the war in Ruthin, after freeing them from the slavery into which the Empire had sold them.

'Was the island empty?' she asked.

'Not entirely, but they were happy to move on for a little gold and a couple of favours. There's nothing here that anyone would want to stay for: there are no decent harbours and hardly any landing sites – a couple of treacherous coves, that's all.'

They anchored a little offshore and rowed across to a tiny beach. A path led inland to a large settlement of at least sixty buildings, set back from the shore and separated from it by a belt of uncleared trees.

'Don't people see the smoke from your fires?'

'Slavers do. They're always looking for easy targets.'

'And?'

'They're not stupid – it doesn't take them long to learn where they're not welcome. It's not good business if they have to fight.'

What he and his men had accomplished here was impressive, considering he had started with nothing. As well as creating the complex itself, he had accumulated substantial supplies of weapons, explosives, clothes and equipment. And there was a significant store of gold, mostly in coins.

'Taken from other people?' she assumed.

'Everything I have has been taken from other people, one way or another.'

Yes, it was impressive, but it wasn't nearly enough to take on the Empire. He knew that, of course, but he still intended to recover the kingdom. So she needed to understand his plans: she had to know whether his confidence was rooted in blind optimism or whether he had a real chance of success.

Now, as she crossed the compound, she felt half the camp watching her: most made some pretence of continuing whatever work they'd been doing, but others simply stopped and stared. She didn't recognise any faces, even though a number must have seen her aboard the *Night Princess*. There, the General's crew had been almost entirely male – Light and Dark Elves – but his forces here were far more diverse. There were women, perhaps one in five, and some Humans.

They would become accustomed to her presence over time, she assumed, but it was pointless trying to avoid their attention now. Instead she tried to seem as purposeful and confident as the General always appeared to be.

The door to the wooden building opened as she approached. He was waiting inside. 'I didn't hear you coming,' he joked, explaining, 'I've never known the camp fall so quiet.'

'They'll get used to me.'

'Yes, they will. But that won't change what they believe – that the Crown of Ruthin is rightfully yours to take.'

'And you're ready to explain to me exactly how we are to take it?'

'Of course, my lady.' He led her through a door protected by two guards, which was an extreme and surely unnecessary precaution on an otherwise unpopulated and remote island. Aravan surely didn't believe that the room needed to be secured so the guards were only there for show, for the effect that they created. Like so much of what he did.

Half a dozen uniformed officers were inside – she had no idea how long they'd been waiting for her. She didn't recognise any from the *Night Princess*, so perhaps Aravan preferred to keep his most senior people away from his ship, either for their own safety and protection or perhaps so that they didn't interfere with his day-to-day activities.

The room was dominated by two large tables, each covered by a map. The first, comprising four individual sheets, showed Ruthin in detail – the terrain and significant features, settlements and major roads. Several dozen pins had been pushed into it, holding tiny flags of various colours and shapes.

'These are where Imperial troops and forces loyal to Duke Struving are stationed,' Aravan explained. 'The smaller pins are where they've been active in the last few months, and where there have been attacks by partisans and reprisals that we know about.'

The other map extended far beyond Ruthin on either side of the Gap: it showed roads and rivers, major towns and an indication of the general terrain. As with the Ruthin map, it was dotted with small flags which she assumed indicated the position and strength of Imperial forces in the region. As she studied it in detail, she realised that the numerous camps that housed refugees fleeing from the conflict were also marked.

However interesting the wider story they told, all these details were only be for context: the substance of Aravan's strategy must rest on the tactical situation within Ruthin itself, so she returned to the first table. 'How accurate is your information?'

'There's a delay, of course, but everything here comes from trustworthy sources: people we've worked with for years and who've been reliable in the past. And a lot of this is fixed: the Empire hasn't changed the basic disposition of its forces for years – where they're based and in what numbers. They cycle the actual troops, of course. Some units are battle-hardened, others mostly untested recruits. We record that information as well.'

'How many are there?' Without knowing what the individual flags represented, she had no way of telling.

'Struving has a thousand men of his own and he employs another thousand mercenaries. Half are in Ravensgill and the rest are spread around the Kingdom. And there are five thousand Imperial troops stationed in Ruthin itself. In theory they're there to support Struving and his forces against local opposition and they're nominally overseen by Struving's men, but in reality they report to Imperial commanders.'

'Seven thousand.'

'Yes. It's not many, but they're not there to fight a war. They're only in Ruthin to keep the population in check and provide visible backing to Struving.'

'But still too many to fight.'

'Fighting would be suicide,' he agreed. 'Not only is Ruthin under Imperial occupation but so are her neighbours, even if no-one admits as much. All the main roads are watched and there are checkpoints, patrols and spies everywhere. If we tried to march in with our thousand souls, they could meet us in the field within a day or two with numbers four or five times greater than our own. Even if our army survived its initial encounter, the Empire can call on substantially more troops from both sides of the Gap.'

'So what will you do instead?'

'We must use small numbers and stealth.'

'You can't defeat thousands of men with stealth. At some point, no matter how long you delay that point, you'll have to face them in battle.'

'I disagree,' Aravan said. 'If we can ensure that the majority of their forces never come into play do that, then we may as well have fought and defeated them.'

'And how will you do that?'

'Every campaign comprises a number of locations that you must control in order to succeed and a number of key enemy resources that you must neutralise in order to achieve that. We dare not face those resources on the battlefield, but it is still possible to isolate them by cutting the routes and methods they use for communication. If they are unaware of our presence, then our control of the battlefield will not be contested.'

'That's how they took the kingdom from my father.'

'More or less. But it won't be as straightforward as eliminating Struving and cutting off communications to the Gate. The Imperial forces will act independently.'

'And we won't have an immense army waiting at the border.'

'No. But we still have a few advantages. The unique geography of Ruthin will be our ally. For all that the kingdom comprises over two thousand square miles, much of that is barren, infertile and barely accessible even during the summer. The habitable land is essentially the long pass on either side of the Ruthin Gap and the otherwise isolated valleys that connect with it, and the majority of the forces that oppose us are based in those valleys.'

Aravan leaned over and tapped a number of the little flags.

'The troops occupying Ruthin are stationed at eleven fortified positions. They're using the two barracks in Ruthin, the fortifications by the Gate and eight strongholds sited in the major valleys. Erindale, Scarth, Summerdene, Oster, Tormendale, Vissdale, Ackerby Cut and Brecken.'

He named them from west to east. Atterlie recognised all the names, but couldn't have pointed them out with any confidence. She hadn't realised it before this moment but in the years since she left Ruthin, her own kingdom had become an alien place to her.

'Your father kept men here and here on the highway: easy to reach and easy to move,' Aravan tapped the ends of two of the valleys. 'But Struving's men have moved further from the main pass – they've done it to suppress resistance along the whole length of the valleys, of course, but it's a defensive mistake because it leaves their communications vulnerable. We no longer need to control the main road to isolate those bases – we only need to control the roads a few miles into the valley, where they are narrow and overlooked. If we can stop alarms and messages from reaching them, then we render them irrelevant without engaging them.'

'For a while.'

'We should only need a few hours.'

Aravan sounded confident, but that didn't mean his plan was a good one. It didn't even mean that he'd convinced himself, since he *always* sounded confident.

'If we do this, there is no room for failure,' she cautioned. 'It is the people of Ruthin who will suffer the harshest reprisals: the Empire won't care whether they had any part in it or not.'

'I know that, my lady,' he said, seriously.

'So what must your small numbers achieve, during their assault?'

'There are individuals who must be removed, and locations that we must control so that our own people can co-ordinate and communicate. And we must occupy certain positions by morning, to reassure the population when they wake – we do not have the numbers to deal with widespread panic. Even though most will support us, there will be some who do not: we mustn't allow them any opportunity to disrupt what we're doing.'

'And once you've achieved all of that, you can march the bulk of the army in.'

'Essentially, yes, though they will have to commit before we are secure. We will not have the numbers to hold these places and people for long.'

'What numbers *will* you have?'

'No more than a hundred. And we'll need a similar number in the days immediately before, to prepare: that's in addition to the people we already have in Ruthin, gathering information. And in case things go wrong, because there *will* be unforeseen problems, we'll co-ordinate with local resistance leaders: people we reluctantly trust.

'Reluctantly?'

'It will only take one informer in their ranks, one traitor, for the entire enterprise to fail. I trust my own people completely, because I have personally vetted every one of them, but I must be suspicious of everyone else. The fewer people who know what's happening, the better our chance of success. It will be a difficult balance.'

'When do you plan to close the Gate?' As soon as it was clear what was happening in Ruthin, the Empire would send overwhelming numbers across the western border – that part of the country would need abandoned, and the Iron Gate closed against it.

'Closing the Gate is the final step: it will alert the Empire to what we are doing, so we must have people ready in place to defend it against a serious assault. But if their garrison has any warning before our men arrive, then we won't be able to close it at all. Worse, they'll send word west to their troops in Summerdene, Scarth and Erindale; and beyond, to the Empire. So it is paramount that we prevent any message from reaching them, just as the Imperial forces did when they took the kingdom from your father.'

Aravan described his plan, its rationale and its risks so easily and fluently that it was obvious he and his men had spent a lot of time agreeing what needed to be done. What he had told her sounded detailed and well-argued, rather than mere fantasy: it might even stand a good chance of success. But realistically, she couldn't judge how practical it was even if they explained it to her at the lowest level of detail. And, of course, taking the kingdom was still only the first step.

'Even if your plan is successful, we don't have enough men to hold the kingdom. Even if every one of your men fights like five.'

'You're right. Once we've seized Ravensgill and the east, we will have to reach some kind settlement with the Empire.'

'You think they'll negotiate?'

'Eventually. They may have limitless reinforcements, but they have finite political will: taking Ruthin is only worth a certain cost and a certain number of lives. Eventually they will relent and come to some accommodation with us.'

'And we can hold the Gate until they reach that point? Once they discover how few we are?'

'In the winter months, yes. I think we can. But we will require support to hold it through the following year, and that brings us to our pressing need for allies.'

'Who *are* our allies?'

'Ruthin's neighbours have always been her strongest allies. Belsace, Rossony, Flax, maybe Erevald.'

'And those kingdoms are already reeling from the war – Belsace and Rossony are wrecked by refugees, rebels and Imperial troops.'

'Because of that suffering, they will feel strongly against the Empire,' one of Aravan's officers suggested.

'Yes, but because of it they have no resources to help us. And the kingdoms beyond them will be even more cautious: they already allow Imperial forces free access to their lands without complaint. And they are small – even if they stand with us, their help would be limited.'

'Individually they are weak, but we are all stronger if we stand together. That's how it has always worked. And there are more formidable forces elsewhere in the Steppes – Darrenby, obviously, and Urenscar: lands whose rulers are not afraid to speak against the Empire.'

'I fear their voices are only strident because there is little risk of any direct engagement with Imperial forces: if that changes, they might suddenly become more circumspect. Besides, their armies may be formidable compared with Belsace or Flax, but against the Empire?'

'There's Corvak, of course,' Aravan added, with a smile. 'But there didn't seem any point in talking to them.'

'No,' she nodded. 'Remember Haroven and Piroven: Corvak and the Empire are two sides of the same coin. Besides, who knows what forces they could actually field.'

Corvak's power was an unknown quantity: even if their Ghost Army was real, it surely existed only for the protection of the Floating Cities and the Church. Of course, if the Priesthood were all trained like the boy Pireon then *they* would be a formidable force. But she suspected that the priests of Corvak would only fight Humans, and even then only for causes that the Gods approved. Not for Ruthin.

'All of which brings us back to Pelledac.' Aravan had mentioned the Confederacy earlier, aboard the *Night Princess*. Since then, she'd considered the idea more rigorously and was even more convinced that it would be a mistake. 'In this struggle,' he continued, 'they are our natural allies.'

'Because we have a common enemy?'

'We do not have to friends to be allies.'

During her travels, Atterlie had heard numerous stories

about the Confederacy – its people and its methods – and most of those stories had not been very pleasant. Refugees from their lands flooded the Three Lands, even more widespread and more numerous than those from Ruthin. She doubted very much that they could be "friends" but their support would bring problems even as simple allies.

'If we used troops from the Confederacy to hold the kingdom then our own people might believe they'd exchanged one occupation for another, and they might be right. And the very presence of Confederacy troops might have the opposite effect than we want. The Empire might consider expending *more* resources, time and lives in order to remove them from its border. The whole area could become no more than a battleground between the two, with neither side sparing much thought for the place or its people. Frankly, if the Empire and the Confederacy want to fight a proxy war somewhere, I'd rather not invite them to have it in Ruthin.

'And thirdly,' she counted the point off on one finger, 'I don't trust them. Whatever terms we agree in advance, who knows what they might ask from us when they are in a position to take whatever they want? If the Confederacy gained some political or military advantage from keeping their forces in Ruthin, it wouldn't be easy to persuade them to withdraw. The price for their help might be unacceptably high.'

Aravan waited a moment in case she had more to say, and then suggested: 'The Confederacy might consider the expulsion of the Empire from the Steppes to be sufficient reward in itself. Not to mention how their reputation and standing would be bolstered by such a victory.'

'Have you reached any agreement with them already?'

'Only an exchange of ideas. Positive, but not with any detail.'

'Then we should step back a little, at least for now. We must maintain good relations with them of course, as with everyone. Assuming we can hold Ruthin without their direct assistance, they would still be a useful counterbalance to Imperial influence. If your plan somehow succeeds, at some future point we will even have to build some relationship with the Empire.'

'Indeed, my lady, and that will be your job as Queen.' She didn't answer, and he continued, 'There is one final factor to consider. There are four Imperial legions operating in the east: twenty thousand regular troops that will pose an immediate threat. Their supply lines and their route home both run through Ruthin, so as soon as we cut those they will march on the kingdom and fight to retake it. Within weeks, if not days.'

'And how will you deal with them?'

'In the time it takes them to react, we hope to arrange some circumstance that will convince them to take a different route home. Our campaign will begin just as winter starts to close in, and that will help focus their attention on supplying their men. We should be able to exploit that weakness.'

She nodded and waited, but the General had finished. 'You have said nothing about either the Keep or Struving himself,' she prompted.

'The Keep is like the Iron Gate, my lady. It could hold out for months unless we have the means and the will to reduce it to rubble. Frankly we have neither. But its strength is also its weakness: it is easy to isolate. If the Duke and his family are shut up inside, then they pose no danger and we can deal with them at our leisure.'

'As long as the Keep holds out, it gives hope to our enemies,' she said. 'Worse, it provides the Empire with a justification to march to Struving's relief, or at least his rescue. If we cannot take the Duke, then those who oppose us will have an excuse to keep fighting.'

'Whether the Keep falls or not will not affect the Empire's judgement regarding the wider conflict,' Aravan disagreed. 'It is not relevant.'

'The Keep is the head, the centre of Ruthin and it will be seen as such even if it has no power. By our own people as well as by our enemies.'

'That's your father talking. The Keep is not necessary, my lady, and we cannot spare the men to take it. I *will* not jeopardise our whole enterprise for the sake of one building.'

'I understand,' she said. 'I will make my own plans for the Keep.'

General Aravan mistook her intentions. 'I am aware of your unique skills, my lady, but endangering your own safety would be madness. If you were to be killed, that would be a serious blow to our enterprise.'

'Rest assured, I'm not intending to storm the Keep myself. I will employ specialist help.' She had a substantial amount of money, enough to pay for an entire army of mercenaries. Even better, she was already well-acquainted with Kiergard Slorn's Company – and they had apparently broken into An'Holt, the Confederacy's famous stronghold.

'That would be a waste of your resource.' The General seemed less opposed to the idea now that he believed she wouldn't be personally involved, though that wasn't exactly what she had said. 'That money would be better deployed elsewhere, my lady.'

'It is neither your money nor your decision, General. And I believe it is important which flag flies from the Keep at the end of that first day.'

'Perhaps,' he conceded, 'but the Keep will be a risky business. Please consult me before you finalise any plans: nothing you do must endanger the rest of our enterprise.'

'Of course,' she promised: 'when I have something more definite.' When they discussed her plans, though, she would be careful to avoid mentioning her intention to deal with Struving herself. Personally.

'Very well,' the General nodded, and they stepped back from his map.

'Aboard your ship, you argued that the continuing struggle was making things worse for the people of Ruthin. Can you be certain that you will not do the same?' she asked him. 'Prolong the bloodshed, ruin even more of the kingdom, set back any kind of recovery even further?'

'Every conflict has consequences,' he told her: 'every conflict destroys homes and families and lives. But sometimes conflict is the only way to achieve your goals. The only consideration is whether you believe those goals are worth the cost.'

'And you think they are?'

'I haven't considered it, my lady. That's a political decision, my lady. I'm just a soldier, doing my duty.'

She laughed at his dissembling. 'I don't think you've been *"just a soldier"* for a long time, and I'm relying on that. Even if your plan succeeds, retaking the Kingdom is going to seem trivial compared with rebuilding it.'

'I will celebrate the day when *that* is our challenge, my lady.'

Chapter Two

Natural Allies

1

According to Halldyn, the rest of the Company had sailed just a couple of days before Lanvik, Kiergard Slorn, Garran and Tyrell returned to Davata Lodge. There was a note from Bane in the lounge: simple and to the point, it explained that they were completing an offer of work. He had left the original letter with it.

'All of them?' Slorn queried. 'Even Magda?'

'Let's hope she doesn't take any stupid risks,' Garran said. They could all imagine Magda pushing herself too hard, beyond what her condition would allow.

'Menska will look after her,' Lanvik said. 'And so will Bane.' Slorn handed him the letter: the job seemed straightforward enough.

Their own trip north had been disappointing.

Kiergard Slorn had fulfilled his friend's last request by delivering a package, but hadn't received any useful information in exchange. Nothing about the people who had been directing Lanvik and the assassin Foxblade to kill – the people who were surely responsible for what had happened to him – and nothing about why. They had already known that the victims were members of some secretive group: beyond that, there was only vague talk of conspiracies and unknown enemies and the woman hadn't committed to updating them if she learned anything more.

Lanvik hadn't even met her: he should have saved himself the trip.

On the road south, they had discussed another possible lead. Given that Lanvik's unknown enemy had also employed an assassin, the Guild must hold some information about their client: they would have received both the contract and the fee, and presumably some method to communicate the outcome back to the client.

'We'll be passing through Arafel,' Tyrell had suggested.

'You're suggesting we ask to inspect the Guild of Assassins' records?' Garran asked. 'Or perhaps break into the Guildhouse?'

'I hope not,' Slorn said. 'Imagine going up against a hundred assassins or more, all like Lanvik's dangerous friend!'

'I wasn't saying that,' Tyrell looked flustered. Being younger, he was still more self-conscious than the others: more sensitive to Garran's particular brand of abrasive if light-hearted banter. 'But I thought maybe Foxblade could find out.'

'Even if we had a way to contact her, it's probably against Guild rules,' Lanvik said.

'I don't think there's any "probably" about it,' Garran agreed.

They all smiled and nodded, but Lanvik resolved to raise the question with Foxblade the next time they met: whether there was any way she could somehow gain access to Guild records. Assuming she was still with the Guild.

Late that evening, he stood and stared at the mirror in his room.

Before heading north, he had been plagued by images in mirrors: he had seen and heard, or perhaps only imagined, his own reflection talking to him. It hadn't happened for weeks, not since they left Calinnia, but he hadn't been looking at his own reflection much: partly as a natural consequence of travelling, and partly through choice. The idea made him feel uncomfortable.

But here, back in his little room, the mirror was unavoidable.

He couldn't help asking his reflection: 'Well? Are you there?'

'I'm always here,' he heard himself say, in his own voice.

'I thought perhaps you'd gone away.'

'No.'

'If you're always here, why have you only been talking since I got this?' He touched the smooth metal amulet that lay on his chest: a gift from the boy-priest Pireon, to "settle" his mind.

'You should take it off,' the reflection said, without answering. 'If you remove the amulet you might not regain your memories, but if you keep it on then I can assure you that you won't.'

'Is that what you need me to do? To take control again? Like before, when you made me kill.'

'Is that your excuse for killing? That I made you do it?'

Lanvik didn't reply: the whole conversation had quickly become awkward. He had an unspoken fear that the longer he talked to his mirror-self, the more power it gained over him. Even if not in reality, then certainly in his own mind. And now he felt that it was trying to goad him into a longer discussion.

He stared at his own face for a little longer without saying anything, and then forced himself to turn and walk away.

Talking to the mirror had been a mistake.

He had largely banished it from his mind during their journey, almost convinced himself that these conversations had only taken place in his imagination. But now they were was much more difficult to ignore.

The voice came from himself, of course: his mouth, rather than the actual mirror. He knew that. But he still couldn't free himself of the notion that there was something physical in the glass, watching him. He couldn't relax and knew that he would find it difficult to sleep, knowing that it was in the room with him. Although he forced himself not to look directly at the mirror, it dominated his attention.

That other persona had only manifested after he started

wearing Pireon's relic, but he was sure that the amulet wasn't responsible. This mirror-talking was some new way for the other Lanvik to reach him, now that he could no longer take control. His other self had only suggested removing it in order to possess his body again.

Eventually he hung a sheet over the mirror before going to bed.

The next few days passed achingly slowly. The four of them were restless and unable to settle to anything constructive while they waited. No-one said as much explicitly, but there was a presumption that the entire Company would set out for Ceran'Don, the Land of Mists, once the others returned.

The Light Elves, both Dog clan, passed their days in weapons training, exercises and sparring. Slorn joined them in the mornings and then headed to a secluded spot inland where he could attempt to coax some reaction from the Ruby Hand.

Lanvik walked in a different direction with his staff, to find his own place to practice unobserved. He still occasionally cast his one spell, if only to reassure himself that he hadn't forgotten it, but mostly he tried to recover others. Now that he had regained some memories of actually using magecraft, he tried to imitate the moves he remembered making. But his recollection was frustratingly incomplete. He could visualise his actions, how he had moved his staff, but he had no memory of any words that he had used or of his state of mind. From his recent experience, he believed there was a specific mental state that he needed to recapture: different for each spell.

He failed so many times, pointlessly repeating the same actions, that his mind wandered easily and he found himself distracted by thoughts of his mirror-self and of his victims and of what might be waiting on Ceran'Don. As a result, he was hardly paying any attention when he cast his magefire. The searing light from his staff sliced a nearby tree in half with a clean, narrow flame. The upper half of the trunk, together with most of the large branches, toppled over and crashed untidily to the ground.

He stared at the tree.

Every time he had used the spell before, it had been indiscriminate and uncontrolled: an all-consuming white rushing fireball. But this new blast had released far less power than previously, and its range and intensity had been equally limited. He walked over to examine the tree: the cut was clean and smooth with almost no scorching around the edge, as if sliced by some immense and incredibly sharp blade.

He had seen the familiar crackling along the staff and felt the usual tingling but he must have done something different this time.

It seemed that his one spell could be adjusted: tailored to a variety of circumstances and requirements. Perhaps it could even be made more destructive, more deadly.

He tried to think back to a moment earlier, but he hadn't been focussed on what he was doing. He cast the spell over and over, but each time it either didn't work at all or else it produced exactly the same uncontrolled result as before.

Damn.

Eventually he trudged back to the Lodge, consoling himself that more of his magic would surely return in the future – though perhaps not as a direct result of his practice and effort. And if he had done this once, even by accident, then he must be able to do it again: he had the power and the ability somewhere within him, even if he couldn't immediately recapture it.

He didn't mention the development to the others, certain that it would create expectations. He would tell them when he had some control over it.

That evening, it was no surprise that his other self was aware of what had happened.

'A little bit more of you has returned,' his own voice observed, 'but you can't control it. You can't remember how, can you?'

'Not yet,' he succumbed to the temptation to reply.

'I know exactly how and I can show you,' his mirror-self said. 'I can show you *everything* you've forgotten.'

'But ...?'

'You have to take off the amulet. I can't show you with words.'

'Even if that's true, why can't you tell me about everything else? Not about my magecraft, but who I am and what happened to me.'

'It's not that easy. I have all your memories, but not as words: I can only pass them on by showing them to you, letting you live them again. To make you whole.'

'If I let you in, how do I know you won't try to take over?'

'You can't know that. Of course you can't. And nothing I can say could convince you. But even if I did, how bad would it really be? There are people waiting for you back home: you have a real family, and friends. A whole life that you've forgotten. A life that you could go back to, if you let me return it to you. Isn't that what you want – to remember who you are?'

Lanvik didn't say anything.

His other self persisted: 'Take the amulet off. Let me come back.'

That surely confirmed that it was the Priest's relic that was keeping him safe from possession. 'Even before the amulet, you weren't able to take over: not completely.'

'No, I wasn't. And surely that must make it safe now, that chance to recover your old self – your old life?'

From the sound of it, neither of them was completely certain what might happen if he removed the amulet. He changed the subject: 'Who are you?'

'You know who I am.'

There was a long pause and neither of them said anything. 'You're me,' he said at last. 'The real me.' He didn't know if it was true, but that was an idea he hadn't wanted to contemplate.

The face in the mirror smiled. 'Yes I am,' it said.

A sudden thought occurred to Lanvik: if the self in the mirror could control his mouth in order to talk, then why not his arm? His hand?

Could he remove the amulet without me even knowing?

Lanvik looked down, reflexively. The amulet was still there, hanging at his chest.

He lay awake that night, unable to sleep.

Was his other self entirely an illusion, created by some sickness his mind? Or was it some projection by an external enemy, no longer able to take control of his body but still able to influence what he saw and heard? Or was it the voice of the real Elidar, as it had claimed, buried deep within him by whatever trauma had left him without memories?

No matter how many times he tried to puzzle it out, he could think of no way to tell which might be true.

Unsettled, he left the sheet hanging over the mirror for the next few days and forced himself to ignore it. He also started tucking the amulet underneath his shirt, so that it couldn't catch on anything: couldn't come off by accident.

Instead he focussed on refining his spell, but with no success.

It was only a few days later that the rest of the Company returned. It was obvious from the way they were walking that something had gone wrong. Lanvik counted them, twice, as they climbed up from the shore: no-one was missing and no-one seemed to be carrying any significant injury.

Slorn was ready to give them time to unpack, but Garran was more impatient: 'Problem?' he asked Bane.

In the absence of Kiergard Slorn, Bane would have been making the decisions – that hierarchy was even more obvious now that Magda was incapacitated. There was Slorn and Bane, and then there were the others.

'It was a trap,' Bane nodded, directing his words to Slorn.

They waited until Thawn and Vander had finished tying up the boat and they were all together in the lounge before explaining what had happened: about the armed men who were waiting, well-organised and trained, and about their escape through the parade in Fodetta.

'We were lucky and they were sloppy,' Thawn concluded. 'We have no right to all be here.'

'I don't know how long they'd been waiting, but they weren't sharp,' Bane agreed. 'They won't make that mistake next time.'

After a long pause, Magda told Slorn. 'There's no point being angry. There was nothing obvious about the letter or the work.'

'What do you think?' he asked her.

'They were all trained and they were all Dark Elves,' she told him. 'They had to be Confederacy. That Death Squad.'

'Armagon Stengiss,' Vrosko Din supplied.

The others nodded: it was the obvious conclusion.

Garran sat tapping his finger on the table. 'It's outrageous that they come here to the Inner Sea, hundreds of miles from Pelledac, and behave like they do in the north.'

'It's what they do.' Thawn had grown up in Avellador, with the Confederacy as neighbours. The last time she'd been home, she'd heard that their agents were operating there openly.

'But this is the Inner Sea,' Garran shook his head. 'And … well, killing monks?'

'You think they killed them?' Tyrell asked.

'What else? Especially if they were Terevarna. I doubt they paid them to leave.'

'Of course they killed them,' Bane said. 'What do you suggest we do about it? Report them to the Guard? If the monks had been in our way, *we* might have killed them as well …'

'It's not important,' Slorn cut across their discussion. 'What happened is in the past now. Perhaps you should have been suspicious about the work, but it was an easy mistake to make. We'll all be more cautious in future. The only important thing is that you survived.'

'The fact we turned up will tell them that their message reached us,' Magda said. 'They'll try to find us through the communication network next.'

'I'll warn Halldyn to take special care that he isn't followed,' Slorn agreed. 'I think he's going tomorrow.' Halldyn visited the nearby island of Stoli every few days, to pick up supplies and check for letters or parcels.

Over dinner that evening, Bane finally raised the question that was surely on everyone's mind. 'Now that we're all here, are you still planning to travel east?' He meant to Ceran'Don.

'For the Glass Sword? Yes,' Slorn nodded. 'Yes.'

A number of the others shifted deliberately in their seats, at best signalling their lack of enthusiasm: more likely their reluctance. The land of Humans and home of mages was not somewhere they would choose to visit. And seeking out the Glass Sword – the whole quest for the Four Trophies – was not the Company's business. There would be no financial reward in it.

'At least the Confederacy wouldn't look for us there,' Garran ironically suggested that Ceran'Don might be a safe destination. A few of the others nodded, more in appreciation of his remark than in agreement with its sentiment.

Slorn spent the following ten or fifteen minutes trying to downplay Ceran'Don's dangerous reputation. After all, they had learned that there were regular ferries; that Elven traders plied those routes. With a larger boat, perhaps they could even sail round the coast to the Eastern Shore and avoid landing at all – there were bound to be charts.

From time to time he glanced across, but Lanvik didn't join in the discussion: over the last few weeks, he had been questioning what he wanted from his immediate future. He felt settled here with the Company, as if he belonged: spending time apart from them had made that more obvious to him. This group of people had become his family and his home. He might have lost his previous life but it seemed that he had made another life here, and that gave him something to protect.

He still wanted to learn who he was, of course: to discover who had done this to him and why, but the notion of regaining his old life was no longer as pressing as before. With the Priest's amulet, he seemed to have shaken free of his most immediate problem: his intermittent possession. And there were the conversations he'd been having in the mirror … regaining his lost memories and perhaps his lost personality might not be the entirely good thing he had previously assumed.

As the evening wore on, he chose not to drink with the others. Or at least, not to drink to the extent that they did. Instead, he sipped at a glass and tried to decide what he actually wanted.

The following morning, he took his staff out to practice before the others woke. Despite his efforts to control his spell, though, it remained identical to when he first cast it back in Amulia.

Magda found him in the quiet dip where he had been experimenting, perhaps a mile inland.

She approached carefully along the higher ground, so that he would see her. Even then, she stopped on a ridge and waved until she was certain she wouldn't be caught by a stray blast.

'Don't worry,' she told him. 'The others might be reluctant now but they'll come round soon enough, if only out of boredom. I know that Garran was joking but after what happened on Comarenza, the Land of Mists is going to feel a lot safer than it did before.'

'Safe from Armagon Stengiss, at least,' he smiled.

'*Safer*, but perhaps not completely safe. Stengiss has shown himself to be very persistent so far.' She looked around, and asked, 'Are you making progress?'

'No,' he shook his head. He didn't want to share his accidental discovery of a few days earlier: not yet.

'And how in the Three Lands are we going to explain this mess to our neighbours?' Their "neighbours" were the population of the only settlement on the island, a fishing village along the shore.

'Sorry.' She was right. Over the last few days, he had turned this little area into a wasteland of churned mud, craters and scorched rocks. 'We need a proper shieldpit,' he nodded, with a smile.

'A what?'

'A shieldpit,' he repeated. 'It's an arena where mages train. The walls are made from ironstone, fused with mage-fire.'

'How do you know that?'

'I don't know.' He didn't remember ever hearing the word, certainly not recently: it had just come to him during the conversation.

'Well I've never heard of such a thing,' Magda said, 'so perhaps more memories are coming back to you than you realise.'

They walked back to the Lodge together, her limp obvious as she negotiated the uneven terrain. He walked at her speed and didn't offer to help – he didn't want to risk making her feel bad: if she wanted assistance, she would surely ask. Like the others, he never mentioned her injuries – acted as if they didn't exist and tried not to stare – but he had noticed most of the Company now found it difficult to look at her directly. Her face still carried several scars, she was missing a number of teeth, and there was a long gash that crossed one of her eyes so that it looked half-closed all the time. He was much happier talking to her like this, walking alongside her.

Late that afternoon, Halldyn returned from Nisia with some supplies for the kitchen as well as three letters.

Slorn looked through them. 'This one's for you,' he held a small white envelope out to Lanvik.

'For me?'

'Yes. I imagine it's from your assassin friend …'

2

While Lanvik carefully opened his letter, Slorn glanced through the other two. They were offers of work, and he put them aside: given what had happened on Comarenza, now was not the time.

If they couldn't take work, was this the end of the Company? he wondered. Why would they stay together if it wasn't profitable? It might be also safer for the others if they went separate ways, he supposed: if they weren't with him. He had no idea.

At first he had been angry that the others had let themselves be tricked, but there was nothing suspicious about the offer: he might have chosen to take it himself, so as Magda had said, there was no point blaming them. There might even be positives to take from this turn of events: to remind him that the Company and this entire life was no more than a means to an end, a diversion.

'Well?' he asked Lanvik.

'You were right. It's from Foxblade.' The Human passed the letter across, so presumably there was nothing personal in it.

Slorn scanned quickly down the single page. She had a proposal that she wanted to discuss in person – that was all. She would wait for them in Vallierta, "close to the harbour-master's office", for as long as she could. She had signed herself "*Vy (Foxblade)*", so perhaps she wasn't entirely sure whether she was an assassin or a princess yet. The date on the letter was less than two weeks previously, so she must have dispatched it from nearby. Perhaps from Vallierta.

Since their first meeting in Haadar, he had been impressed with the girl. Her abilities were exceptional, both in close combat and in reconnaissance; and although she was no Magda she had some skill at opening locks. He had already suggested she join his Company, but there was no mention of that in her letter.

'Well?' Bane asked.

'She wants to talk. She has a proposal.'

'Does she say what it is?'

'She doesn't need to,' Magda said. 'We know what she wants – she wants us to become involved in the Captain's grand plan to "liberate" Ruthin.'

'Well, that's nothing we want anything to do with,' Garran said.

'It's a hopeless cause,' Bane agreed. 'And it's not the kind of work we do – political; high profile; high risk.'

'We should at least hear what she has to say,' Lanvik disagreed.

'She wants to meet in Vallierta, which is where we saw her last,' Bane had glanced through the letter. 'So she may be concealing her movements and the Captain's from us. If she's protecting him, how closely do you think their interests have aligned? How much can we trust her?'

'I don't think her loyalties are to Captain Redwolf, if that's what you mean,' Lanvik offered. 'Her loyalties are to herself and then to Ruthin. The Captain and his plans come third.'

'From what I saw, *you* might well come third,' Magda disagreed, 'and the poor Captain a distant fourth.'

'I think you're being needlessly suspicious,' Vander said. 'She's chosen Vallierta because she knows it's convenient for us. That's all.'

'I agree,' Thawn said. 'I think we can trust her.'

'Are we going?' Bane asked Slorn – it was his decision to make.

'Perhaps Lanvik should go,' Slorn suggested. 'We're not going to get involved in anything political, but we should stay friendly.'

'I'm going anyway,' Lanvik said. 'She's a friend.'

'You hardly know who she really is,' Slorn reminded him.

'I don't think friendship depends on how well you know someone,' Magda said.

Slorn smiled hesitantly. 'Try to remember that she's an assassin, at least, and don't just trust what she says.'

'She's more than an assassin,' Lanvik said.

'Yes, she's also a princess. But I don't think that makes her more trustworthy. Probably the opposite.'

'She deserves to have her say. And whatever she has in mind, she can pay well.'

'She also knows who we are and what we do,' Magda agreed. 'I don't think she would waste our time.'

'A few of us will go and meet her,' Slorn conceded.

'What boat do we use?' Bane asked.

He was right – they had no idea if *The Thieving Priest* had been compromised. It was difficult to see how she wouldn't have been. A few simple enquiries would have turned up a description and name, together with details of her crew. And if the Death Squad had access to Confederacy intelligence and their regular military then they had eyes and ears in every major port around the Three Lands, including Vallierta. So they would learn that the Company had landed there, and when.

Just a few weeks before, *The Thieving Priest* had cost them over four thousand Crowns – a fortune. And now she might be useless.

'We can't just buy another boat,' Lanvik said, practically. 'Can we?'

'Well we can't sell this one,' Thawn said, flatly. 'We can't risk leaving a trail.' That was why Slorn had insisted they scuttle *Magda's Choice*.

'We can't afford to keep replacing our boat, not if we can't trade in the old ones.'

'There's not much that's unique about her,' Vander said. 'There's no hurry, so we could repaint her, refit the deck and give her a new name: she wouldn't look like the same boat at all. And then we could sell her.'

'If we did all of that, it would be simpler just to keep her,' Magda said, 'if we really thought it was safe.'

'Perhaps,' Slorn agreed. 'But we don't have time to do any of that now.'

'We can decide what to do about the *Priest* when we get back,' Vander suggested. 'We should borrow a boat, just for this trip. There are plenty at the village.'

He was right: at least a dozen sizeable fishing boats sailed out of Calinnia. Slorn doubted that they were as large as the *Thieving Priest*, but the whole Company wouldn't be coming.

'I'll ask Halldyn to sort something out,' he agreed. There were several locals working on extending the jetty and he could have talked to them himself, but Halldyn would have a better idea of who could help. If something could be arranged quickly enough then they could leave tomorrow or the day after.

As they ate that evening, a dark blue fishing boat bobbed slowly into the bay. After tying up opposite the *Thieving Priest*, a couple of her crew helped Halldyn give the vessel a thorough clean for her new role. None of the Company could generate any excitement or interest in the boat, so no-one even walked down to examine her in any detail.

It wasn't until the next morning that they took a good look at what they'd borrowed – or rented, rather, since there had been an accompanying financial transaction.

Because the jetty was only partially complete, they had to edge along struts and balance on temporary boards just to get close. There had been no chance to disguise the boat as anything other than an old and rather worn fishing boat, but Halldyn had given her on a new name in case they ran into trouble again – *Erribel*.

Slorn wondered who Erribel was or had been.

'It stinks of fish,' Thawn complained. She'd brought a small bag of things, like the others, but seemed reluctant to lay it down anywhere onboard.

'It's a fishing boat,' Garran shrugged. He had come to see the others off.

'But Halldyn must have spent *hours* cleaning it yesterday,' Vrosko Din screwed up his face. Slorn's retainer had worked on the boat well into the night.

'Imagine what it smelled like before, then.'

The smell didn't deter Vander at all – he walked the length of the deck, had a quick look at the masts and the sails and turned the wheel from side to side. 'She'll be fine,' he reassured the others.

Six of them would make the trip – along with Slorn and Lanvik, Bane and Thawn were coming in case of trouble and Vander and Vrosko Din had volunteered to join them. Ethryk and Menska were both happy to skip an unnecessary sea voyage; Magda felt she would be a liability; and the others had shown little interest in the trip.

Slorn had no idea of the size of her usual crew, but the boat felt tiny. The bulk of the vessel was given over to the hold: even removing the nets and other equipment still left a large space that couldn't be used for anything else. The six of them were restricted to the deck, a tiny galley and two cabins that were packed tight with bunks.

Out on the open water, *Erribel* seemed to bob up and down and roll from side to side at least as much as she moved forwards, so the unpleasant journey seemed to take forever.

When they finally reach Vallierta, Lanvik appeared disheartened that his friend the assassin was not waiting at the quayside.

'It's a large port,' Bane told him. 'There's no way she could watch every arrival.'

'And she certainly wouldn't be expecting us in this boat,' Vander added.

'She'll be waiting in a klava house nearby,' Lanvik said confidently. 'I'll go and find her.'

'Wait,' Slorn disagreed. 'We should be a little cautious.' His instincts told him that the assassin would not have tricked them, but the Company's recent experience had left him more wary than usual. Even if she had come in good faith, Redwolf might have sent people with her: he didn't particularly distrust the Captain, but he wouldn't expect any special treatment if their interests were ever in conflict. So before they looked for Foxblade, he had Thawn, Bane and Vrosko Din scout out the harbour as discreetly as they could for anyone acting suspiciously who had military training, whether from Ruthin or the Confederacy.

They returned after ten or fifteen minutes.

'No-one,' Thawn said. 'Or at least, no-one obvious in the immediate vicinity. But it's a big place – it wouldn't have been hard to miss someone.'

'Fine,' he nodded. 'Let's get the paperwork out the way then.'

In smaller coastal towns and villages, locals usually directed crews to the harbourmaster's home. Larger ports normally boasted a dedicated harbourmaster's office: a simple hut that was manned for a few hours each day. By contrast, since Vallierta might see several hundred boats arriving or leaving on any day, the "harbourmaster's office" was a two storey building that ran for half the length of the main wharf and boasted at least a dozen offices, each with its own entrance. The majority of the administration dealt with the loading, unloading, inspection and taxation of cargo vessels, but there was still a lengthy queue just to register private boats and pay berthing fees.

After completing the paperwork, they acceded to Lanvik's suggestion that they check the nearest klava houses: they found Foxblade in the eighth establishment they visited. She was sitting at a corner table, facing the door, playing cards with Elisha of Giren Pass.

Slorn stopped when he caught sight of Elisha, frozen for a moment.

Aboard Captain Redwolf's frigate *Night Princess*, he had asked her to join his Company and she had told him, 'There's something that I have to do first, something more important than my passions. You know that.'

'I could help,' he had suggested. 'I could come with you, for a time at least. The road is always safer for two than for one.'

'Don't worry about me. I've never found the road dangerous,' she said. 'Thank you for your offer, but ask me again when my life is my own.'

He didn't fight the smile that came to him now. She stood as he walked over, also smiling as if they shared some private joke. They touched hands when they were close enough. Slorn wasn't even sure which of them had made the first movement.

'I didn't know you were here,' he told her, though a part of him had been secretly hoping for exactly this. He often thought of her when he was alone, and his imagination played out scenarios in which they met and talked. More than once, he had worried about this obsession – worried that his mental image of Elisha might be his own creation rather than the actual person. But here she was, exactly as he remembered her, and just the sight of her had made him happy.

'I wanted to come,' she explained. 'To see you again.'

'And the Captain let you?'

'The Captain was happy that I wouldn't be alone,' Foxblade offered. 'I keep turning down his offer of bodyguards.'

'Have you been here long?' Lanvik asked.

'A couple of weeks.'

'That's a lot of klava.'

'We haven't *just* been sitting here drinking klava,' Elisha said.

'No, but mostly.'

'Do you have somewhere we can talk?' Slorn asked. 'Somewhere private?'

'Not private enough for our discussion, no,' Foxblade shook her head. 'I assumed that we would go aboard your boat.'

'Fine,' Slorn agreed. That was the safest choice as far as he was concerned. 'Let's go.'

'I think we're probably going to finish our game first,' Elisha said. 'And our klava.'

'So what will we do until then? Spectate?' Bane asked, annoyed.

'It's not a problem,' Vander said.

'I'll have a klava,' Lanvik agreed.

So the five of them sat at another table, talking among themselves. It was more than an hour later that they set off back for the *Erribel.*

'Which one is yours?' Elisha asked, as they walked along the quayside.

'The blue one,' Slorn pointed.

'The blue one? You said you were buying a new boat, but that wasn't what I thought you meant,' Foxblade said. 'I wouldn't have guessed it was yours, so I suppose it's an effective disguise.'

'This is just temporary,' Vander told her, awkwardly. 'There's a problem with our own boat.'

'What kind of problem?'

'Our Confederacy friends may have identified it. We had an unfortunate encounter with them.'

'Was anyone hurt?'

'No.'

'Only because we were lucky,' Bane said.

'This is a conversation for when we're aboard,' Slorn interrupted, uncomfortable at how freely they were discussing the Company's business in the open.

Thawn greeted them with a wave as they approached and helped them up on deck.

'We should go inside,' Lanvik suggested. 'It's private. But a lot smellier.'

They pressed into one of the cabins and the corridor immediately outside, so that everyone could hear what Foxblade had to say.

'You already know that General Aravan has designs on the Kingdom of Ruthin,' she started. 'Captain Redwolf, as you know him. He has a detailed and specific plan to drive out Duke Struving and his sponsors in the Empire. I'm in broad agreement with his plan, but I have a number of additional goals that he is unwilling to commit resources to.'

'So you need your own people to achieve those goals?' Slorn prompted. 'People under your command, not his.'

'Yes. People I can rely on.'

'And you're happy to say all of that in front of his agent here?' Bane asked her.

'Elisha already knows why I'm here, as does the General. I doubt he expects me to abandon my priorities any more than I expect him to abandon his.'

'There won't be any conflict, then?' The Company enjoyed a good working relationship with Redwolf and the last thing Slorn wanted to do was jeopardise any future collaborations.

'No.'

'So what are these goals that you believe are important and the General does not?'

'I am convinced that we should take the Keep in Ravensgill, and detain or otherwise remove Duke Struving and his family. It might not be a tactical priority, but it would be an important symbol.'

'A symbol that might help the people of Ruthin better appreciate where their loyalty lies,' Slorn understood.

'Exactly.'

'I'm not familiar with the Keep in Ravensgill.'

'It's the oldest part of the palace; the traditional home of the royal family. It has a single door and small windows: none on the ground floor. Ruthin has been at peace for centuries, but the Keep's security has never been compromised for comfort or convenience.'

'What's your assessment?' Slorn asked her. He appreciated her skills at breaking into buildings as well as evaluating their defences.

'There's no easy way in. The Keep has its own water supply and enough supplies to withstand a long siege. There are no separate entrances for servants or deliveries. It's at more or less the highest point in Ravensgill, so it's not possible to overtop its walls or even look down on it. The walls are too thick to easily or quickly blast through, and there is no part of its immediate surroundings that cannot be fired upon from within. In addition, the rock that it's built upon on is hard and dense – tunnelling by hand would be nearly impossible.'

'Windows?'

'Tiny – a young child could pass through them: I did when I was eight, but I was small and skinny. So the only way in or out is through the door. And finally, there's a garrison stationed just outside the palace grounds, not more than three or four minutes away.' She smiled: 'Within Ruthin, the Keep is widely reputed to be impregnable, but they say that about An'Holt.'

'So how do we get in?' Lanvik asked.

"We"… he's already agreed to this.

'I assume by deception, but the details are up to you,' she said. 'I've heard you can employ inventive and daring strategies as well as simply blowing things up.' She had only seen the Company work in Q'ushar, where they had employed significant quantities of munitions to attack targets across the town.

'And this is a financial proposition?' Bane checked. He would also have noticed Lanvik's "we".

'Entirely,' she said. 'I'll pay you whatever sum we agree.'

'I'll help,' Lanvik told her, sincerely. 'I'll do whatever I can.'

'So will I,' Vander agreed, which was more of a surprise.

'We haven't decided that we're actually doing this,' Slorn said. He had come here to be polite, but essentially to dismiss the assassin's proposal. He had priorities of his own. 'This is not really the kind of work we do.'

'We do all manner of work,' Vander disagreed.

'And we normally decide as a group,' Lanvik said.

'The others are trusting the six of us to decide,' Bane said. 'Isn't that why we're here?'

'So what *have* we decided? Do we vote on this?'

Damn.

It was an awkward situation: Vander and Lanvik were clearly in favour of helping, and he guessed that Thawn might be as well. He and Bane were against it, and Vrosko Din had said nothing. In this small group, the best outcome was probably a stalemate.

He could try to force the issue of course, but here in Vallierta there was a good chance that Lanvik might simply leave them and go with the assassin. And if that happened, who knew whether Vander or even Thawn might choose to accompany him.

He shouldn't have let the Human come, he realised. That had been a mistake.

And now, he needed to avoid a vote.

'You're right,' he nodded to Lanvik. 'This is a decision for the group to make: everyone should have a chance to make up their own minds. We should take them back with us.'

'Both of them?' Bane queried. 'Why would we trust this woman?' He meant Elisha. No-one had explicitly said as much, but they all trusted the assassin.

'It won't be a problem,' Slorn said.

'Your judgement is clouded,' Bane advised. 'Even you must recognise that.'

'She'll report back to the Captain,' Vrosko Din said. 'Where we are, what we say, what we do.'

'I don't think she will,' Slorn disagreed. 'I trust her.' He felt embarrassed and annoyed that they were having this conversation in front of her.

'Maybe you think that, yes, but isn't that another decision we should take as a group?' Bane said. 'Our safety is at stake as well.'

'Will you report everything we say to Captain Redwolf?' Thawn asked Elisha directly.

'Not everything. But I *will* tell him whatever I think he needs to know.'

Thawn stared at her impassively for a long moment, before nodding. 'That's fair.' That answer had apparently settled the matter for her.

'It'll be fine,' Vander spoke up unexpectedly. 'I don't think she means us any harm.'

While Slorn appreciated his support, the boy seldom thought *anyone* meant them any harm. The others shared his sentiment though, judging by their indifferent responses. Apart from Bane, everyone was willing to trust Elisha – at least to some extent. While she and Foxblade fetched their bags, however, they agreed that Vander would take a more circuitous route back to Davata Lodge to better conceal its location. The village of Calinnia itself would be too identifiable as a landmark, so they would approach from the north.

The journey back passed quickly. He spent the time with Elisha, talking: the fishing boat was neither conducive nor private enough for anything more than that. Since none of the others complained about their flirting, though, they took that as a licence to continue.

When they arrived back, they tied up alongside their new ketch.

'*The Thieving Priest*,' Foxblade read. 'I like that.' She had been travelling with them when the boy-priest Pireon had stolen the Emerald Crown.

Lisamel, Tremano and Garran walked down from the Lodge to greet them and, no doubt, assess their two passengers. They walked casually but were armed. Slorn saw Tyrell standing just up the hill, in the shadow of the Lodge.

As if oblivious, Elisha breathed in deeply as she stepped down onto the jetty. 'This is nice,' she said. 'Quiet.'

'And it doesn't smell of fish,' Foxblade added.

'It does a little,' Garran greeted her. 'You can't get away from it on the coast'. He turned to Elisha and asked bluntly, 'Why are you here? Did Redwolf send you spy on us?'

'Of course he did, but I'm also loyal to my lady Vy'Rhienn.'

'Their interests coincide for now, of course. Let's hope you don't have to choose between them.'

'Yes, let's hope so,' she agreed, and then added, 'The others decided they could trust me.'

'Trust you enough to bring you here, at least,' he pointed out. 'Who knows whether they'll trust you enough to let you leave again.'

'They came back with us so that everyone can hear what the assassin has to say,' Slorn interrupted Garran's sparring. 'It's something we have to decide on.'

Magda was waiting up at the Lodge: she still hated being slower than the others. 'I'm surprised you brought Elisha,' she said, when they were close enough.

'Slorn's decision,' Bane said.

'I assumed that, yes.'

'She says she's loyal to the Captain *and* the Princess,' Garran interjected.

'She probably is,' Magda nodded, 'but I don't see how that helps.'

'It's late,' Slorn said. 'We'll eat before we hear Foxblade's proposal.' He paused. 'Vy'Rhienn's proposal.' He kept thinking of her as the assassin, but Elisha had addressed her and referred to her in terms of her new identity – or rather her *old* identity, he supposed. He should probably make an effort to do the same.

'Piastamo's in the kitchen,' Halldyn said. 'I warned him that you might be back today, but didn't know about the extra two.'

'I'm sure he'll manage,' Slorn said.

It was only half an hour later that drinks and the first few platters started arriving. The princess watched as various dishes were arranged on the huge table in the lounge. 'You lead a very comfortable life, for mercenaries,' she remarked: 'Not exactly what I imagined.'

'You thought we'd be holed up in a cave somewhere?' Garran asked. 'Scavenging for rats?'

'More or less,' she shrugged, with an easy smile. Slorn remembered how detached she'd seemed when they first met – how much more like an assassin. He wondered whether the change had come naturally now that she'd left the Guild or if she'd spent time practising: from what he knew of her, very little of what she did was spontaneous.

They avoided the topic of her proposal while they ate but as they relaxed afterwards with a few bottles of wine in the evening light of spring, it was Vorrigan who asked, 'You're here about Ruthin?'

Vy'Rhienn nodded, seriously. 'Of course.'

She explained, carefully and without much emotion, what she'd already told the others in Vallierta. There were a handful of obvious questions so the discussion took almost an hour, and then she emptied her glass. 'I assume you'll want to discuss this without me here.'

'Without either of you here,' Bane agreed.

'Then we'll go for a walk. And perhaps unpack.' Halldyn had already opened one of the outbuildings for the two women and taken their bags there.

Slorn half-expected arguments to start immediately after they left, but there was silence around the table. People picked at morsels of food or refilled their glasses.

'Well?' he prompted.

'Considering the risks, it would make more sense to avoid Ruthin completely,' Tremano said.

'Everyone else in the Three Lands seems to be steering well clear of the place,' Lisamel agreed.

'We'd probably be safe from Armagon Stengiss,' Garran commented.

'Like Ceran'Don, then,' Menska said, drily. 'Though I'm sure he'd be happy if we went to either, assuming he wants us dead.'

'To be fair, it surely wouldn't be much more dangerous than a lot of what we've done in the past,' Ethryk said. 'Day to day life in Ravensgill can't be that bad: despite the refugees, most of the population still lives there. And taking this "Keep" must be easier than rescuing Magda from Q'ushar.'

'This is political,' Lisamel said. 'I didn't think we did "political".'

'When you came for me in Darkfall, that was political,' Vander said.

'No, it wasn't,' Bane said. 'It became political later.'

'I didn't think we cared if the work was political,' Thawn said. 'All we care about is how much it pays, don't we?'

'And Foxblade can pay extremely well,' Lanvik added.

'She'd have to, for work like this,' Bane said.

'How difficult can it be?' Lanvik asked. 'Compared with An'Holt?'

'You weren't even there,' Bane said. 'People died.' He avoided looking at Vander: the loss of Aruel still affected the boy deeply.

'Perhaps we could scout them out – Ruthin and the Keep,' Thawn said: 'Get an idea of how bad things there actually are.'

'I'm sure she'd pay us for our time,' Lanvik encouraged.

'That would only take a few weeks,' Ethryk nodded slowly. 'Paid weeks. And we can just walk away if it looks too difficult.'

'I don't think it will be *difficult*,' Slorn said. 'The problem is that the country's in the middle of a very unpleasant war, a war which we're going to become part of.'

'And we're relying on Captain Redwolf's plan having at least some measure of success,' Bane pointed out. 'Otherwise we'll be badly exposed.'

'How much of a problem would that be, working around Redwolf's timing?' Magda asked.

'I don't know. We don't normally work to other people's schedules.'

Garran snorted: 'Almost everything we do is according to someone else's schedule. That part of it doesn't bother me. But how does this fit in with Slorn's schedule?' He was talking about the trip to Ceran'Don, the Land of Mists, to pursue Lanvik's past and to search for the third Trophy – the Crystal Sword.

Slorn didn't respond: given the others' lack of enthusiasm for that project, he'd already been thinking that he might have to pay them to do it.

'Personally, I'll go to Ruthin first,' Lanvik said. 'Foxblade is my friend, so nothing that anybody says here really matters. Not to me.'

'I'll help her as well, if I can,' Magda said, unexpectedly. 'I have a lot of sympathy for her, and there's nothing wrong with doing something political. Compared with a lot of what we've done, this is almost noble.'

'Noble?' Slorn echoed. It hadn't occurred to him to consider the assassin's proposal in moral terms.

'Well, yes. Unless you think what the Empire's done in Ruthin is acceptable. And in Belsace. And Rossony.'

No-one else spoke up, so it was difficult for Slorn to gauge what they were thinking. 'Does anyone else have something else to say?'

No-one said anything.

A few shook their heads.

'In that case, there's no point prolonging the discussion. I'm sure most of us need some time to think about this, so I think we should sleep on it. We'll sit down again in the morning.' The delay would give him an opportunity to talk with some of the others privately and perhaps influence their opinion.

Everyone nodded and leaned back from the table. The Company broke into smaller groups: some went to get cards, others alcohol or spiceweed. A few of them, no doubt, would continue discussing the assassin's proposal among themselves.

Slorn wondered if he should talk with Magda. On an issue like this, that would normally be the first thing he did: discuss it with her, ask for her views and what she thought the others would say. In this particular case, she seemed quite clearly in support of the proposal whereas in his mind it was at best a distraction and at worst dangerous.

He also had to consider the cohesion of the Company: if the others supported going then he would need to fall in with that decision, even if his heart wasn't in it. The notion that they functioned as a single team, despite any disagreements, would make it easier to persuade them to accompany him to Ceran'Don afterwards. If they survived Ruthin, of course.

'Someone should tell our guests they can join us again,' he suggested.

'I'll go,' Lanvik said.

From one of the upstairs windows, Slorn watched Lanvik walk towards the little outbuilding that Halldyn had made up for their visitors. Elisha emerged before he reached it, they exchanged a few words and then she headed down to the shore. Slorn watched her standing at the water's edge for a few minutes until Magda joined him: 'She's probably waiting for you.'

He took a jacket down to the little beach as an excuse, as if he needed one. 'I thought you might be cold.'

'It never gets cold here, in the Inner Sea. Not properly cold.'

'Sometimes it snows,' he told her, 'but not very often.' He pointed back up to the Lodge. 'We didn't reach a consensus. We'll decide in the morning.'

'Yes. That's what Lanvik said.'

She hardly knew any of them, but already seemed to have a more comfortable relationship with the Human than with the others – he often had that effect, though Slorn was unclear why: people chose to like and trust him. Of course, Elisha's opinions might have been swayed by his close relationship with the assassin.

Despite what she said, she took the jacket and pulled it round her shoulders. 'It's nice here. Better than nice.'

He nodded. Their conversation was stilted, but that didn't matter.

They meandered slowly along the shore, just above the line where the waves washed the sand in tiny ripples. And then they returned to the Lodge, took a bottle out onto the upper terrace and a couple of hours later they both retired to his room. There was no discussion or question about it and it didn't seem to surprise any of the others.

Later, after everyone else was asleep and the Lodge was quiet, she asked, 'What will you do about my lady's proposal?'

'We'll decide tomorrow.'

'I meant you – what will *you* do? Whatever you decide is going to carry more weight than anything the others say.' She adjusted her position slightly, half-turning against his chest; and his hand slipped down from her shoulder to rest on her side. He could feel the contours of her ribs under his fingers.

He didn't say anything, until she eventually prompted, 'Well?'

'I don't know,' he admitted.

'You have doubts?'

Did you come here to persuade me? On whose behalf – Aravan's? Or the assassin's?

'Honestly, I think the entire adventure will most likely fail. A few hundred men against the Imperial army?'

'Perhaps the Gods favour our cause.'

'Dimir's teeth, the Gods would need to fight alongside you if they want you to win,' he told her. 'And what if they favour your enemies? They normally favour the side with the largest army.' She didn't reply, and after a while he added, 'You know that you don't have to get involved.'

'What do you mean?'

'Leave it to the princess and the general – it's their campaign, not yours. You could stay here with me. You could join my Company.'

'This is my war just as much as theirs. You know that. Ruthin is my home, and I will do whatever I can to avenge Oric.' Oric had been her pairbond, tortured and murdered by Duke Struving's men. Slorn found the mention of her previous relationship unsettling: unsure how he should feel about it and how she wanted him to react. She rubbed his chest gently with her fingers, as if to reassure him: 'The way I feel for you doesn't mean I've stopped caring about him. How could I …?'

He changed the subject: 'I wish there was a safer way for you to do this. I don't like the idea of you putting yourself in danger.'

'Thank you.' From her voice, he knew she was smiling. 'Though you're not really in a position to speak. Not from what I've heard.'

'Perhaps not,' he admitted.

They didn't talk after that and she quickly fell asleep, even in a strange bed with unfamiliar company.

He lay awake for a long time beside her, thinking.

Outside, he could hear the quiet noises of the night – the lapping of waves; sea creatures quietly surfacing to breathe; the wind rustling through the longer grass. He briefly wondered if he should have posted someone on watch, perhaps Garran, but there wouldn't have been any point. Of their two visitors, Elisha was here with him and if the assassin wanted them dead then a lone guard in the darkness wouldn't stop her.

Damn her.

What she was proposing was both risky and unnecessary. Nothing more than a dangerous diversion.

Ever since taking possession of the Ruby Hand, his intention had been to travel east to Ceran'Don in search of the Glass Sword. Now that Lanvik was back with them, there had never been a better time: it was almost fortuitous that the Company's activity around the Inner Sea had been constrained by their Confederacy hunters.

But Lanvik was suddenly less enthusiastic. He almost seemed to welcome the assassin's proposal as an excuse to delay, and Slorn had no idea why he had lost his principal ally. As far as he was aware, nothing had happened during their weeks in the north that might have affected the Human's state of mind.

Perhaps the amulet wasn't as effective as it had first seemed: perhaps the influences on him were not completely neutralised after all and were still sapping his determination. If that was true, of course, Lanvik might still be dangerous to those around him.

Slorn forced himself to set that thought aside, for now.

Despite Lanvik's loyalty to the assassin, Slorn was certain that he was still committed to rediscovering his past. Even if he had temporarily cooled to the idea, they were imperfect allies in the matter. Imperfect because Lanvik's goals in the Land of Mists were unconnected to Slorn's and his priority would surely be finding answers about what had happened to him. Privately, Slorn believed there was a high chance that he would wander into the middle of some mage conspiracy that he didn't understand and end up dead and no use to anyone.

It would be essential to persuade him to help with the Glass Sword before that happened: they surely couldn't travel around Ceran'Don without at least one Human in their party. And if he used his only spell to help them, then he would be the most useful member of the Company. Unfortunately his willingness to wield magecraft was even more limited than his memory of how to go about it.

Setting aside Lanvik, none of the others held any enthusiasm for a trip to Ceran'Don, understandably enough, though he was sure they would come round to the idea. Their reluctance didn't automatically mean they favoured this venture in Ruthin, of course. Some had spoken in favour of it, but a number were against it: Bane, most clearly; Vorrigan; Lisamel and Tremano; and Menska's only comment had been quite negative.

Of those who supported the idea, Magda's voice would carry most weight with the others tomorrow. But if Slorn spoke against it then they would mostly follow his lead, he hoped. Except for Lanvik. Lanvik would go with the assassin whatever the others agreed, so regardless what Slorn decided, the Human would not be travelling to Ceran'Don until this business was complete.

That in itself was a powerful argument for the Company to travel to Ruthin: just to keep Lanvik safe until they needed him.

And if he was completely honest, Slorn himself was starting to have doubts that the Trophies would help him the way he had hoped. For all their reputation as the most powerful weapons in the Three Lands – the weapons of the Gods, no less – he had failed to trigger any reaction from them. The seasons were rushing past and he wasn't making any progress. It would soon be a year and a half since he had taken the Crown: time that he had lost forever. And all that time, his Imperial Father was becoming weaker and weaker. At this rate, Silvendor would ascend the throne before Slorn was even ready to make his own bid for it.

Although he had been pinning his hopes on the Four Trophies, in his heart he knew that using them had never been more than an optimistic dream, borne of desperation. Borne of a simple lack of other options. The fact that he had retrieved two of them was astounding, he supposed, but he had been unable to use either. And he had now lost one of them again. For all that, he hated the idea of delaying the journey to Ceran'Don. After all, the Glass Sword was an actual weapon: the legends and the mysteries celebrated its destructive powers.

And however imperfect, mastering the Trophies was still the only real plan he had.

Except that … perhaps … his brother wasn't the only one who could employ magecraft.

Now that Lanvik possessed a spell, he was surely as good as an army. As good as any of the stupid Trophies, if they wouldn't work. He might not be able to persuade the Human to his broader cause, of course, but there were apparently ways to control him: ways that the boy priest from Elagion understood something about.

But, if that was to become his new strategy, then Lanvik recovering his memories and returning to his former life would be a disaster. So that would be a reason *not* to rush to the Land of Mists …

At this moment, nothing was clear: everything was in balance and no particular course of action seemed better than any other.

Except that, from any dispassionate perspective, the Ruthin adventure was foolhardy and dangerous: the Company should obviously not become involved with it, despite the assassin's offer to pay them as if it was a normal piece of work. They might not all come back.

Imagine if I was killed or wounded in this stupid operation.

But again, things were not straightforward.

He had to think about Elisha now.

The situation in Ruthin was so important to her that he found it difficult not to care about it himself, as if their feelings for each other had created a kind of emotional sympathy between them. A resonance. And he couldn't shake the uncomfortable fear that she could easily die in Ruthin, given the inevitability of her becoming directly involved in the struggle to come. The forces supporting her cause were badly outnumbered and the Imperial Army would show no quarter, especially after ten years of this vicious war.

She surely had no real idea how slight their chances of success were, or how bad things could get. Even if she had, he doubted it would temper her resolve.

From a practical standpoint, nothing that the Company did for Foxblade was likely to affect the outcome of Redwolf's broader campaign. But if they were there, in Ruthin, then at least he would be close by in case Elisha needed help.

He realised that he had already made his decision, lying there in the darkness.

Despite the fact that it risked everything he had worked for, he was going to go to Ruthin, not for the assassin but for Elisha. But he wasn't going to rush in blindly, led only by his emotions.

For a start, if Redwolf really had a detailed plan then he wanted to see it.

In his experience, staunch patriots with a noble cause were normally the worst at judging the merit of their own plans. And the best at getting other people needlessly killed.

Chapter Three

The Tears of Ardendar

1

Dach and Dasha's shared ceremony would take place at Kayoden's principal Temple about a month after the equinox, sixty-five days after Quiron's announcement, and there would be a large reception afterwards near the centre of the island. It would be a social and political event, so it made more sense to make use of the island's civic buildings rather than the family estate. It was a family occasion as well, of course, but Pireon anticipated seeing far fewer of his relations than at their Majority. That had been the first gathering of the wider family for several years, whereas this would be the second in quick succession: many would feel no need to demonstrate their allegiances and loyalties a second time. He was expecting the estate to be much quieter.

He had invited Iera again but she declined, again, and he hadn't mentioned it after that. He wouldn't be able to persuade her by simply asking over and over again. If she changed her mind then she would tell him. She had said nothing, though.

Dach and Ajiila left two days before him so he travelled home on his own, as usual.

Despite the estate being less busy, he was given a room in the attic again. Amphet and his family had been displaced from the north house, but on this occasion they took up rooms on the second floor. Dach and Ajiila were meanwhile promoted to one of the grander first floor suites. He first spotted them when he arrived, deep in some discussion with Uncle Quiron, and he waved from a distance rather than interrupt. Dach called back, 'Talk to you later!'

He chose to pay a call on his Great Aunt Uthraiche instead, but she wasn't in her rooms. One of the staff suggested that she might be with his grandparents, so he returned to his room and practised his ritual devotions until dinner.

That evening, they all ate in the Grand Dining Room, thanks to a few additional tables. There was no seating plan: Ajiila and Dach chose to sit with the senior members of the family; Pireon sat with Amphet, Ilada and their children.

The room was a jumble of voices around him but even so, as everyone arranged themselves, he heard his grandfather Ephander's voice commenting, 'That's Timo's little boy. The Priest. They say he's the youngest Priest-Acolyte ever. Certainly in living memory …'

He couldn't help smiling to himself. It seemed that he might have been forgiven for wearing his cowl and overshirt to the previous family dinner: on this occasion, no-one remarked on his clothes at all. The two months since they had last seen him was apparently enough for both the family and the staff to become comfortable with how he chose to dress.

Deon, Amphet's older boy, pointed out Ajiila's parents to him: they had arrived from Irriandor the day before, together with her younger brother. 'I like him,' Deon offered. They had apparently spent most of the day playing together.

Ajiila had mentioned her brother several times, but Pireon had to think for a moment before suggesting, 'Ulnior?'

'Yes, that's him,' Deon agreed.

There was nothing about either of Ajiila's parents to suggest where she inherited her striking looks: on the contrary, they seemed almost plain. Their clothes were smart but rather dull, as if their main purpose was not to offend, but they didn't seem at all overawed by either the occasion or the company. While they talked with Quiron and Dasha, the boy Ulnior sat and toyed with the food on his plate. He was clearly bored and was making no effort to disguise the fact.

'He should have sat with you,' Pireon suggested.

'Yes, he should,' Ilada agreed, 'but it's too late now. We'll suggest that in future.'

After the meal, while everyone else milled around, the two boys met up and ran around the gardens shouting and laughing. When Amphet told them to quieten down, Deon asked, 'Can we take one of the skiffs?'

'It's getting late.'

'It's still light, and we won't be out for long. Just along the coast a bit. Maybe to the ferry pier.'

'I can go with them,' Pireon offered.

'Well, alright then.'

'Thanks, Uncle Pireon,' Deon beamed

Uncle Pireon?

They were away for about an hour and Pireon had to row them back, as the boys claimed their arms were tired and sore. He said very little throughout but listened to the boys sharing increasingly improbable tales about their past adventures and those of their friends.

Ajiila's parents met them at the jetty.

'Thank you for looking after them,' her father said, as the boys ran off.

'I'm glad to have something useful to do,' Pireon admitted, tying up the skiff. One of the staff would come down later and return it to the boatshed.

'You're Pireon, aren't you?' her mother asked, as they walked up to the main house. 'Ajiila pointed you out at dinner.'

'That's right,' he agreed, wondering what she had said.

'She always mentions you in her letters, right from when she started on Elagion. And she used to talk about you all the time when she came home.'

'Nothing bad, I hope.'

‘Oh, never anything bad,’ the woman assured him, seriously. ‘You introduced her to Dach, didn’t you?’

‘Yes,’ he agreed, trying to keep any hint of bitterness from his voice. ‘Yes, I did.’

‘You’ll always have our thanks for that.’ She took his arm in hers and they walked like that as far as the terrace.

Pireon spotted Dach and Dasha at one table, and made his excuses.

‘Sit down,’ Dasha greeted him. ‘We’re waiting for Ajiila.’

‘I see you met her parents,’ Dach said, before admitting: ‘I’m always a bit nervous around them. I never know what to say.’

‘Pireon always knows what to say,’ Dasha smiled. ‘Even when the right thing to say is nothing at all. And that’s something you never got the hang of.’

‘You’re the one who never shuts up,’ Dach protested.

‘So anyway,’ Dasha ignored her twin and turned to Pireon, ‘you came alone again.’

‘Yes.’

‘If you want to bring Iera sometime, you know she’s more than welcome.’

‘She doesn’t travel very well,’ he said, feeling acutely embarrassed but without knowing exactly why.

‘Well, I’d love to meet her. Ajiila says she’s very nice.’

Again, it somehow felt awkward and inappropriate to be talking about Iera that way. *Why am I being so childish about this?*

‘Yes,’ he forced himself to say, seriously. ‘I think she is.’

He felt much better from having said that and knew it would be a little easier to talk about her in future.

Before Dasha could press him further on the subject though, Ajiila joined them. She had changed clothes since dinner. ‘Sorry, I got held up,’ she apologised. ‘I was talking to your Great Aunt. The one with the funny name.’

‘Uthraiche,’ the others chorused.

'That's right,' she laughed. 'And I just saw my parents on the way out,' she told Pireon. 'They couldn't stop telling me how nice you are! What in the Three Lands did you say to them?'

'Em, nothing I think. I was just polite.'

'You see,' Dasha said to Dach, and they both laughed.

'What did I miss?' Ajiila looked between them.

'They were joking earlier about how Dach always talks too much,' Pireon explained.

'Well, that's about right,' Ajiila said: 'sometimes he doesn't know when to shut up.' She kissed Dach on the fore-head and asked, 'Why does no-one have a drink?' She looked around and waved to one of the staff.

They passed the rest of the evening in relaxed and inconsequential conversation. After Dasha left to be with Quiron, other guests intermittently came over offer their congratulations and best wishes to Dach and Ajiila.

The following morning after breakfast, Ajiila and two of the staff took the family launch to collect her mother's parents from the East Harbour. The old couple had travelled at a more leisurely pace from Irriandor, staying overnight at the dam.

Pireon found himself supervising the two boys again. They were playing with model boats when the launch sailed back into the little bay. As Ajiila helped two older Madarinn onto the jetty, Ulnior ran to greet them: 'Arva! Etta!'

'We're at the right place, then,' the woman reached down and squeezed the boy's shoulders.

'Here, I'll get those,' Pireon offered, as Ajiila started lift-ing a number of bags across from the launch.

'Both of you! Leave those bags alone!' an imperious voice commanded. Vialta had come down from the house without him noticing. 'You're not on Elagion now.' Then she addressed the new arrivals: 'Welcome to the Kayoden estate. I hope your journey wasn't too uncomfortable.'

'It was lovely,' the woman assured her. 'I just hope we didn't hold anyone up.'

'There's plenty of time to settle in and change,' Vialta assured them.

'Do you want something to eat first?' Ajiila asked.

'Heavens no, girl,' her grandfather said. 'We've only just had breakfast.'

'And I'm far too excited for food,' her grandmother agreed.

'We have a room for you on the first floor,' Vialta interjected: 'if you'd like to come with me.'

'I'll show you,' Ajiila skipped beside them. 'I've seen it already. It's lovely, and it looks over the lake.'

Ulnior accompanied the group up to the main house and Deon trailed after them, leaving Pireon to retrieve the little wooden boats they'd been playing with. He noticed that the wind was stiffening; dark, threatening clouds had appeared on the horizon.

He offered a quick prayer to Heklash that the dry weather would hold for the ceremony, and followed that with a similar prayer to High Belluhar: Heklash was one of the more fickle and less dependable Gods in the Pantheon. Perhaps one of them had been listening, though, because as the family and guests gathered at the main gate two hours later, the skies were clear and there was no hint of rain.

Kayoden's principal Temple to the Dead God was faced with white marble, with unusual detail in black and green. It sat almost at the centre of the island and was its largest Temple by some degree: although nothing like the size of the Mother Temple on Elagion, it could still hold a thousand or more.

Dach, Dasha, Quiron and Ajiila would enter from the front with the Priests, but everyone else filed through the main Temple doors at the back. A number of areas at the front had been roped off for the immediate families and there was a row for the senior household staff, but the rest of the building was packed. Even the side chapels.

Amphet had organised the seating plan, and stood near the entrance directing everyone.

'You're beside Aunt Uthraiche,' he told Pireon. 'Everyone knows you get on with her, so you have to make sure she doesn't make a scene.'

'Oh, thanks.' Pireon said, wryly. He had no idea how he could have stopped his Great Aunt from saying or doing anything she pleased.

When she arrived, he escorted her slowly down the centre aisle. 'So you're to keep an eye on me, are you?' she asked.

'Something like that,' he admitted.

'Well, as long as I don't have to sit next to Ephander …' She pursed her lips. 'My brother can be insufferable on these occasions. But at least they won't make any trouble about the girl.'

'Ajiila?'

'Exactly. They like her. She'll encourage Dach to settle down and make something of himself. And she won't be any challenge to them.'

Pireon bristled at his Great Aunt's casual slight, but he didn't react and she didn't say anything further on the matter. She was probably right.

Once they had taken their seats, she became preoccupied with her own thoughts and memories and Pireon was able to get a good look at the inside of the Temple as he waited. There were echoes of his family everywhere – decorations and emblems, colours, plaques and inscriptions. They even had a small private chapel to Tohros – Healer of Souls and God of study, science and philosophy. And of water, of course, so Tohros was widely worshipped across the Lakes.

His family's influence on this space was not surprising: the principal Kiritas estate was on Kayoden and they had been the Temple's main sponsor for centuries. He wondered what happened in those cities where two or even three of the Great Families were established: did they each support a different Temple? Or perhaps they made specific agreements about contributing to the same space.

The noisy rustling and background chatter fell abruptly silent as three Senior Priests walked out from behind the altar. The Primate of Kayoden would officiate, and one of his assistants was to be the old priest who presided at Dach and Dasha's Majority. A few seconds later, Uncle Quiron and Dach were led out from one side, and Ajiila and Dasha from the other. It was odd seeing his brother and sister standing there. And Ajiila. Whenever he thought of them, he always imagined them as younger than they were now: not as adults.

To his eyes they seemed somehow out of place.

Once the sacrament started, he was relieved that the Primate instilled the occasion with a sense of pomp and grandeur, helped by the incense in the air and the fact that the tiniest sound echoed around the Temple itself and its great dome – the space that belonged to the Gods. The Majority had left him worried that the ceremony might be stilted and awkward: a shadow of what it could have been.

He noticed that Dasha was wearing the gold bracelet that their mother had left her, and his thoughts turned to the little cloth he had received at the same time. He had carefully re-sealed it, in the hope that it would retain her lingering scent for longer. Among his handful of personal belongings, it was the most precious, even though he might never open it again for fear that its fragrance would be lost forever.

He was consumed by a sudden deep regret that their parents hadn't lived to see this moment; hadn't lived to see their children bond, or even see them growing up. Lost in contemplation of his parents, his childhood and his family, he paid very little attention to the sacrament itself. It seemed to pass so quickly that he felt slightly guilty at the end that he would have very few memories to take away.

A number of slightly showy carriages were waiting outside to transport the principals and their immediate families to the reception at one of Kayoden's civic halls. Most of the guests walked through the centre of the city: the crowd of several hundred, many of them Kayoden's finest, attracted a number of curious stares.

The venue offered a large courtyard at the back, accessed from the main hall, but the air outside had turned chilly and it was largely empty. Musicians played in two of the three rooms and, although there was an impressive quantity of food laid out on tables along the walls, the majority of people chose to dance or simply stand talking rather than eat.

A tall, muscular Madarinn about Pireon's age approached him: he recognised the man from Dach and Dasha's Majority.

'Pireon, isn't it?'

'That's right.'

'Kyraeos,' he introduced himself. 'Kyro.'

'You're Aunt Ialyssa's son, aren't you?'

'Yes, I am. Well done. Most people remember my mother but hardly anyone remembers me.'

'I have the same problem with my brother,' Pireon smiled ruefully. 'They're both very memorable. Is she here?'

'No. As usual she's tied up with politics and administration. I suppose I should be as well, but it doesn't hold my interest as much as she wants it to.'

'So this is a convenient excuse to escape your responsibilities?'

'Not entirely. I have a list of things to do for the family while I'm on Kayoden.' Kyro meant the Thireos family that Ialyssa had bonded into, another of Corvak's eighteen Great Families.

They talked together for about twenty minutes, enjoying each other's company despite having very little in common beyond being related: like his mother, Kyro projected a slightly ironic outlook, unusual for Corvak. He excused himself eventually: 'Anyway, I can't stand here chatting to you and enjoying myself. I need to do a bit more mixing.'

'Under orders?'

'Always,' Kyro agreed ruefully. 'Like I said, I have a list.'

'Give my regards to your mother.'

'I will,' he promised, and then disappeared into the crowd.

Although Pireon recognised hardly anyone, he was frequently greeted by name as he wandered through the rooms. He must be one of the easiest guests to recognise, he supposed, on account of being the only one dressed as a priest. Except for the three priests, of course, who he was avoiding.

He found most of his immediate family standing outside, despite the chill, and joined a little group that included Quiron, Dasha, Dach and Ajiila.

'Congratulations, all of you,' he said. He hadn't talked to them since before they left the estate.

'Thank you, Pireon,' Ajiila beamed at him, and then added, 'Little brother!'

Dach squeezed her waist. 'Don't tease him.'

Standing nearby, he saw Ajiila's parents in a group of people he recognised but couldn't identify – some of his distant relatives, presumably. And her grandparents were talking with Amphet and his family; the boy Ulnior was with them.

Not for the first time that day, he was struck by the fact that his mothers' parents – his other grandparents – weren't there; hadn't come. They certainly wouldn't have been invited, of course, and it was quite possible that they had no idea that two of their grandchildren were now pairbonded.

The more he thought about them, the more bizarre that whole situation seemed: the notion that one side of the family could so completely shut out the other. He knew better than to raise the subject, but Ajiila had no such conditioning.

'Why aren't your other grandparents here?' she asked Dach, bluntly.

Dach looked startled by the question, just as Dasha had been when Pireon suggested that they should have been at her Majority. 'We don't get on,' he explained. 'We don't talk. Or see them.'

'Wouldn't you want them here anyway?'

'That's a strange question,' Dach frowned.

'No, it's not a strange question at all. It's normal for your whole family to be at your bonding,' she insisted. 'If my father's parents were still alive, they'd have come.'

'If they ever wanted to see us, they know exactly where we are.'

'Well, they're your family too. I'd love to meet them some time.'

'You'll have to arrange that yourself,' Pireon warned her. 'Nobody else will.'

'Pireon!' Quiron scolded.

'Oh, don't spoil things, Pireon,' Dasha glowered at him.

He shrugged, but at the same time promised himself, *I will visit Alaion and talk to our grandparents. Soon.*

Carriages had been laid on to transport the family and their houseguests back to the estate. It would take a number of trips, though, and a large group chose to walk instead, Pireon among them.

He hadn't properly seen the streets of Kayoden since he'd been very young, and then only in the company of adult servants. He looked at the city through different eyes now and everything seemed smaller than he remembered: smaller and more ordinary. Bland, even. Dach might have ambitions of being posted here when he left Elagion, but

Pireon realised that he didn't. Kayoden was pleasant enough, but it was a backwater. How could anything of any value be accomplished in a place like this?

He smiled at his own hubris, at the idea that he would *accomplish* things in his life, let along accomplish things *of value*. If Iera could have heard his thought, he knew she would have laughed and teased him.

It started spitting with rain just before they reached the estate but the heavy downpour that had threatened all day held off until the last wave of carriages, arrived a few minutes after they did. As the staff hastily brought in the chairs and tables from the terrace, Pireon offered a short prayer of thanks to Heklash. And then to High Belluhar.

There was music in the ballroom but no-one was dancing: instead, people drifted in and out of the public rooms in small relaxed groups, chatting.

Just as there had been at the reception, there were tables of seemingly endless snacks. Pireon hadn't eaten properly since breakfast and, like everyone else, picked away at a little of whatever was available. He had discovered a particular weakness for spiced ellermeat, which was served in small parcels of sweet pastry: as the evening progressed, he found himself returning to the buffet tables every few minutes, telling himself that each time would be the last.

As night began to fall, a tight pain in his stomach told him that he'd probably eaten too many.

He found a bowl of iceleaf on one of the tables and stood looking out one of the downstairs windows as he chewed on a few leaves to ease his indigestion. Hindera was low in the sky behind the main house, casting dramatic shadows across the grounds. Her cold blue light made ever-changing patterns ripple on the low waves of Lake Olchos beyond, speckled with the reflections of the stars.

From the house, it wasn't possible to see the family memorial – the quiet corner of the grounds where commemorative stones were placed for those who had died – but he found himself looking in that direction anyway. Among the stones were two for his parents, with a shared inscription beneath them:

No longer with us but still together,
running and laughing,
dancing in light,
among the tears of Ardendar

Those words were like an echo of his father's letter, and its curious expression:

"If you want to see us clearly, step back, look up and count the tears of Ardendar"

He was still unconvinced by Dasha's explanation that the words were a metaphor, paraphrased from some poem that he had never read, but she had explained to him that the "tears of Ardendar" referred to the redwether flower, because of the colour and the shape. If the letter had a hidden meaning, he wondered where he could find redwether flowers. Why would he count them? And what secret would that number reveal?

He stared out at the darkness for longer than he had intended: the iceleaf was tasteless in his mouth, long since sucked dry of flavour, and the house behind him had become much quieter. There was no music, only the murmur of a dozen conversations. Most people had retired to bed.

He left the soggy remains of the iceleaf on a plate and then couldn't resist detouring by the buffet tables one last time, where he picked up the three remaining ellermeat parcels.

As he lay in bed, drifting off to sleep, he puzzled over the "tears of Ardendar".

Was his father referring to an emblem or a motif somewhere? A flag? A design inscribed on a book cover, perhaps? A book with some message inside, waiting for him.

Or maybe there was some everyday object in the house that resembled a redwether flower?

As he dozed, he dreamed of secret places where he might discover a last message from his parents, though none of his imaginings included any detail of what such a message might say.

The next morning, perhaps because of all the spiced ellermeat, Pireon felt lethargic and heavy. He woke unusually late and was one of the last down for breakfast. The dining room was half full of people talking quietly while they sipped at klava or fruit juice. A number of people acknowledged him when he came in, but he chose to sit alone.

He hadn't eaten properly the day before and was hungrier than usual, so he took a bowl of porridge and covered it with fruit jam. Before even starting, he prepared a second plate, heaped with cooked meat, eggs and pastries.

He was just finishing the porridge when Amphet's little girl, Yuna, came into the dining room. She collected a plate of toast and three small bowls of honey and carried them over to his table.

'Hello, Uncle Pireon,' she said, sitting down and pouring herself a glass of water.

'Are your mum and dad not eating?' he asked.

'We were here before,' she told him. 'But I wanted more toast and honey.'

As they ate, it was clear that Yuna actually had very little interest in the toast but was simply spooning honey into her mouth. He wondered whether he was supposed to be responsible for her, as an adult. Like with the Novices.

Vialta arrived in the dining hall, perhaps called by one of the serving staff, and rescued him from his dilemma. She walked straight over to their table and said, 'You've probably had enough honey now, don't you think?' Then she took the spoon out of the girl's hand, and explained, 'If you eat any more of that, you'll make yourself sick.'

'Yes, Vialta,' Yuna agreed.

'Now, let's go and wash your face and hands. You're all sticky.'

Pireon watched them leave, hand in hand.

Vialta hadn't said anything to him, but he imaged her silently rebuking him for not intervening. Even though he lacked any specific responsibility, he doubted that excused him from not acting. At least, not in Vialta's eyes. Not for the first time, he found himself reflecting that life was much simpler when all the rules were written down.

After eating, he stepped out onto the terrace. It was still cloudy but the rain had stopped: the ground was wet and muddy.

"If you want to see us clearly, step back, look up and count the tears of Ardendar"

Well, he decided, he couldn't lose anything by taking his father's instructions literally and doing just that. He walked across to where the stage had been erected for Dach and Dasha's Majority. The grass was damp underfoot and slightly spongy, and he felt his feet sinking slightly into it with every step.

When he was standing exactly where he had first read the letter, as near as he could tell, he took a step back and looked up … secretly hoping to somehow see redwether flowers.

Of course, he had no idea how far up he should look, exactly. Up to the sky? Or across at the house? The roof, maybe.

It didn't matter where he looked, though. There were no redwether flowers.

Instead, he found himself staring at the side of the ballroom. Ironically, of course, its windows *were* shaped like flowers: marindell flowers. Each of the house's large public rooms had been designed and decorated according to a single theme, with windows shaped to match.

Then he suddenly realised what should have been obvious from the start.

It might not be possible to see redwether flowers from here but it certainly was from the other side of the house, because the library had windows in the shape of redwether flowers.

I'm an idiot. A complete idiot.

He ran round the outside of the house, almost slipping on the wet ground in his excitement, until he was facing the library windows.

He could hear his heart pounding as he counted them.

There were six: six identical windows in a row.

He counted them again. Six.

He had counted the Tears of Ardendar. That was what his father had asked him to do.

And the answer was six.

But how was that significant? What did six flowers mean?

Dejectedly, he reflected that he hadn't even needed to run through the mud. He could probably have counted the library windows from memory: he'd sat in there enough times.

Except …

Except that now he thought about it, the library didn't have six windows. The library had *five* windows. When he imagined himself sitting inside, looking out at the grounds: there were only five windows. And that meant – that meant the library didn't stretch as far as it looked from outside.

The only way there could be six windows on the outside and five on the inside was if there was a whole extra room, somehow hidden away.

Surely there couldn't be.

He wiped the mud off his sandals and entered the house

through the south door, walking along the corridor to the library. He stopped in the doorway and counted the windows, slowly and deliberately. There were five.

The missing one was on the north side, towards the centre of the house, so the wall which should have separated the library from the south stair must actually separate it from some other, hidden space.

But how could he get inside that room?

From the corridor? Or from the library.

His heart racing, he walked across to the north wall of the library and paced slowly along the shelves there, intermittently pulling out books out and knocking on the wall behind them in case it sounded hollow.

'Have you forgotten how to open it?' One of the household staff, Taellis, was standing in the doorway behind him.

'Yes,' Pireon said, puzzled.

Taellis walked over and reached round the side of the shelves second-closest to the window. 'Here,' he explained: 'there's a little catch.' There was a deep click and then he simply pulled: a section of the wall, complete with shelves laden with books, swung out and revealed a small room beyond.

Pireon ran his hand along the side of the shelves, becoming familiar with both the catch and the mechanism, and then stepped into the room. There was a desk at the window and a chair behind it, facing out across the grounds. Apart from the empty shelves that lined the back wall, the only other furniture was a faded armchair.

'Does everyone know about this place?'

'I would think so, yes. Most people.'

Why would his father leave a coded message directing him to this little room if it wasn't at all secret? Had he somehow misunderstood? Or perhaps Dasha had been right: there had never been a message and Pireon's imagination had simply run away with him.

'Did my father use this room?' he asked.

'Oh yes. This was his study. He used to work in there, but it's empty now. Your uncle had all his papers cleared away after he died.'

So the room had been important to his father, at least.

'Thank you.'

After Taellis left, Pireon sat down and stared out at the gardens. Perhaps the secret wasn't in the room itself, but something that was only visible from this chair. But he could see nothing remarkable: nothing that he hadn't seen a hundred times before from elsewhere in the grounds or from other windows on this side of the house.

He pulled open the desk drawers, one by one. Not only were they all empty, but the bottoms had been broken – as if someone thought they might have been false. As he explored further, he also discovered that the back panel of the desk had been cut all the way across; the cushion of the seat had been slashed open and then repaired; and the bookcases had been pulled away from the wall and then repositioned. Someone had been searching very hard through his father's things.

The little room hadn't been "cleared". It had been ransacked.

At her Majority, Dasha told him that Quiron had been looking for their father's notebooks, but was his Uncle really so desperate to find them? What did he think was in them? He couldn't ask Dasha, he realised – he didn't trust her to be discreet. And he couldn't ask Quiron directly: if he *had* been responsible, he would surely deny it and the question would only serve to alert him to Pireon's interest.

Perhaps he could talk to his Aunt Ialyssa. She had spent her childhood here on Kayoden and would have had known Timo and Quiron well. She surely didn't have a vested interest in any ongoing quarrels or family politics any more, not now she'd left, so anything she said would probably be more trustworthy and honest. That idea wasn't very practical, though. He couldn't simply sail to Enixis and interrogate her, and if she hadn't come to Dach and Dasha's bondings then he wasn't likely to run into her at any future family occasion.

He sat back down at the desk, and wondered who his father had needed to hide things from? Who was it that he didn't trust, to the extent of leaving a coded message for his children?

Of course, the message was still a puzzle: surely his father couldn't have hidden anything of value here, where everyone knew he worked? This little room would have been the first place anyone looked – judging by the damage, it *was* the first place they looked.

Even more uncomfortably, Pireon began to wonder about the circumstances of his parents' death. He knew almost nothing beyond the simple fact that they had drowned: he had only been two years old at the time, of course, and had always felt awkward about asking anyone.

But perhaps it was time he found out.

2

She stood to leave, but Director Rabeth said: 'Jetta, could you wait behind.' It wasn't a question.

'Of course, Director.'

She hated Rabeth's familiarity – they had never been close enough for him to know her as "Jetta", but she smiled and said nothing. The Leader called her that, of course: that was his way. But it was a hundred times more annoying from a self-important functionary like Rabeth.

All that the Leader would know of this meeting and countless others like it was what the Director chose to tell him, and that made his position a dangerous and powerful one. As a result, the man thought he was far more important than he was: Jetta supposed everyone despised him for it, at least a little. At best he was capable, nothing more – the kind of person who was always appointed to such a role: lacking both the imagination and the ambition to take full advantage of it.

Around twenty people attended the weekly Eastern Shore Policy group, so the room took a few minutes to clear. The others around the table gathered their things and spun off into secondary discussions: mostly nothing more than personal pleasantries. Honnet D'Vall from External Security remained seated. And Wyke. The Military Council was an almost inevitable presence – in a "monitoring capacity", usually, which was a transparent euphemism for snooping. The Council liked to believe that they were the real power in the Confederacy, and that would be a difficult fiction to maintain if they didn't know what was going on.

Rabeth hadn't spoken to either D'Vall or Wyke, which meant that the discussion to follow had been agreed with them before this morning's meeting.

Nice to be in the loop ...

As Joint Head of External Affairs she attended half a dozen weekly meetings like this one. The role had been presented to her as essentially diplomatic, but she increasingly thought of herself as a bureaucrat: all she ever seemed to do was sit in meetings.

To all intents and purposes, this was a demotion. She had never been directly blamed for the debacle at An'Holt, but she couldn't escape the rumours. Few people knew exactly what had happened, but it was undeniable that it had happened on her watch. Worse, she had actually been there at the time – the evidence of that was written across her scarred face.

Her childhood friend Nemendir Tarq had been Base Commander at the time, but he largely escaped censure. His long-planned promotion to second in command of one of the strategic assault groups had conveniently reduced his visibility. Despite being posted to some remote base in Umbrol, she was certain that he'd be happier there than running An'Holt: he had seemed elated that something had actually happened there, no matter how bad it had been.

The Leader himself had created this new post for her. She had a delicate touch, he told her: a subtle understanding. She would be more useful to the Confederacy in this position, a new role for which he didn't want someone with a military background. This role would be an opportunity, even though it wouldn't be at Ministerial level – in fact, she wouldn't even run a Department. She would become a Joint Head, sharing the responsibility with two colleagues. She would have special responsibility for the Steppes and the East and they both knew how important the Steppes would become as the Perina Canal neared completion.

The Leader had also made it quite clear that she had no option but to accept.

Hundreds of people reported to her, but most of them hardly set foot in Pelledac from one year to the next. She managed dozens of Embassies and Consulates, each of which was staffed with diplomats and administrators, as well as hosting the usual mix of trade envoys, military observers and spies. She co-operated closely with External Security, in that they provided her office with funding in exchange for operational assistance.

Despite that, she was now less privy to what their people found out than in her old Ministry.

To date, her role had principally comprised attempting to placate their neighbours in Ellior, Outhen and Avellador, which was both pointless and thankless. The Confederacy *had* to act against the various rebel groups operating out of those kingdoms: if their own security was tighter and they co-operated more fully with their neighbours to the north, then there wouldn't be any problem.

That particular message was difficult to convey without sounding like a bully.

In reality, both sides knew perfectly well that the Confederacy *was* bullying them and would continue to do so for the foreseeable future. But neither side could speak that particular truth without a good deal of precisely the kind of unpleasantness that it was now her job to prevent.

On the plus side, she didn't have to authorise torture any more. Or supervise it.

The meeting room had emptied and the chattering in the corridor outside slowly died away. Rabeth closed the door. Whatever extra business their impromptu discussion concerned, she hoped it wouldn't detain her too long. She had an appointment later with an old friend, on a more personal matter.

The four of them kept their seats from the earlier meeting, despite the spaces between them.

'External Security has an update concerning Ruthin,' Rabeth started, 'and the Leader believes this would be an opportune moment to review our policy regarding the kingdom as well as our own operations on the ground.'

'One of the former royal family seems to have surfaced,' D'Vall explained. 'This has altered the dynamic of the conflict and appears to be accelerating the plans of various groups. We now expect a significant attempt to overthrow the current regime to occur either in the latter part of this year or next summer. If that fails, it's unlikely that the will or the resources would support another attempt for at least a decade, so this would appear to be an opportunity nexus.'

An "opportunity nexus", Jetta resisted the temptation to smile. *Founders!*

'Who is this new claimant to the throne?' Wyke asked.

'One of the young princesses.'

'Where have they been hiding her? And why haven't we heard about her before?'

'Her appearance has surprised the rebels as much as us. She apparently presented herself to the army in exile and has allied herself with them.'

The "army in exile" was a remnant of the former armed forces, based in the Inner Sea and well-resourced. They both funded and directly undertook covert operations in Ruthin, including targeted attacks, information gathering, assassinations and the dissemination of rumours, misinformation and broader dissent. They had made contact with the Confederacy some seven or eight years previously.

'The girl is genuine?' Jetta asked.

'They think so,' D'Vall nodded. 'Or, at least, they're acting as if they think she is.'

'They've also stepped back from us recently: cooled a little, for no obvious reason,' she supplied. 'That could be the result of a new voice in the leadership.'

'According to our sources, they've been contacting a number of Ruthin's former allies across the Steppes,' D'Vall agreed. 'That would tally with a shift in their approach.'

'Are they having any success?' Rabeth asked.

'No-one's committing to anything, certainly not publicly, but that's hardly surprising. Some level of logistical or financial support may still have been pledged, but probably no more than that.'

'In that case why would they turn away from us?'

'She's probably worried that our terms will be too high – political influence or economic concessions,' Jetta suggested. 'They haven't completely broken off communications, though: they're keeping their options open.'

'But we've lost influence?' Rabeth asked.

'It certainly sounds that way,' Wyke nodded.

'It's difficult to say exactly what influence we had before. We certainly never committed to anything more than money and arms, in case we needed to deny there were links,' Jetta disagreed. 'But if this news is true then the Empire's hold on Ruthin might come under real pressure, perhaps for the last time, so we should be doing whatever we can to support that effort rather than worrying about how much influence we have.'

Rabeth nodded: 'You're right, of course. It would be of almost incalculable value if the Empire lost control of the Gap, regardless of any loyalty or future concessions or agreements we might gain in the process. Can we convince them that our support comes with no strings attached?'

'I doubt they'd believe us,' Jetta told him. 'This is political, after all. Even admitting it would weaken our position with them.'

'Do we have other resources that could influence the outcome?' He looked at D'Vall and Wyke.

'We have a dozen people operating in Ruthin and the kingdoms immediately to the east of it,' D'Vall said. 'They're jointly funded,' he indicated Jetta, 'so it's not clear exactly who has authority over them.'

'I don't think we care about the funding,' Rabeth said, slightly sharply. 'What do they do for us?'

'Mostly they gather information, but we've also used them to channel equipment, training and weapons to the local resistance,' Jetta said. She had read the files on their operations just last month. 'Nothing that can be traced, of course.'

'Good. So we have direct connections with some of the local forces?'

'Connections, yes, but not much influence. It's difficult to get leverage over people who would fight anyway, with or without our weapons and our gold.'

'Fanatics?'

'Patriots.'

'But will these "local forces" be involved with this new actor, this princess?'

'If there's any kind of popular uprising then yes, we would expect a high level of engagement,' D'Vall said. 'The various factions loosely work together already.'

'We must do whatever we can to help close the Gate to the Empire, within reason,' Director Rabeth said. 'As long as it's nothing too overt.'

'We can send more arms or money if they request it,' D'Vall suggested. 'But I don't see how we can do more than that.'

'We could insert a unit of our own,' Wyke suggested. 'Not with any specific remit, but standing ready to assist if required. Over the border in Belsace, perhaps. Undercover.'

'We would have to be very careful,' Jetta pointed out. 'If something like that was discovered, it could set back our operations in the area by years. And not just with the Empire.' The Military Council usually lacked subtlety: it was sometimes difficult to disguise a hammer, particularly when it was proud of being a hammer.

'And it's easy to forget how suspicious a large group of Dark Elves can appear, across the rest of Mehan'Gir,' D'Vall added. 'Can I suggest that the Council works with External Security on this. We have more experience of putting people in the field and keeping them hidden until they're needed.'

'I want you two to explore that option,' Rabeth nodded. Technically, he might have no seniority over the others in the room, but his judgements were effectively direct instructions from the Leader's Office. 'Will you need additional funding?'

'The Council can cover the cost of the operation,' Wyke offered.

'Excellent,' the Director stood, smiling. 'Every day that goes by, I'm more confident that this fourth century will mark our greatest triumph. The balance of power in Mehan'Gir is tilting in our favour, my friends, and it will never be dragged back. To the Future!'

'The Future!' they echoed.

Rabeth walked away alone, a wad of papers under one arm.

Jetta exchanged a few words with Honnet D'Vall: gave him a name to liaise with and a promise that resource and support would be available if required. The respect that came from her reputation at Internal Security wouldn't last forever, so it was important to cultivate as many fresh links as she could. There was no telling what she might need in the future.

Despite her apprehension, their discussion hadn't lasted nearly as long as it might have done. She still had plenty time to stop at the Ministry to drop off her notes and her coat – the day was now much warmer than the morning had promised.

The Ministry of External Affairs was a relaxed and altogether more welcoming structure than the headquarters of Internal Security. It boasted a roomy interior and a leafy courtyard at the centre, though its two stories made it a dwarf among the administrative buildings of Unity Boulevard. She enjoyed the surfeit of space that was a consequence of so few members of the Ministry physically working in Pelledac.

For the first month, she had shared the Secretary's old office with the other two Joint Heads. That space was now a meeting room, and three new and almost as generous offices had been provided instead: these were sufficiently remote from each other that most of the staff could easily be divided to suit. Her responsibility for the Steppes and the East in fact required more resources than either of her colleagues, who were responsible for the Five Seas and the South, and the Northlands and the West.

Outside the Ministry, few people were entirely sure precisely what her position entailed and that lack of clarity had largely worked in her favour so far. She had very few direct responsibilities, but had inserted herself in a wide variety of operational and policy groups across government, particularly those involving the Military Council, External Security and her own former Ministry. Her responsibilities had never been defined precisely, but she assumed that she would be rebuffed if she reached too far beyond her remit.

That hadn't happened yet.

She left the Ministry and walked towards the shore. She could have flagged down a carriage, but preferred to walk through the city on such a bright, dry day. She felt comfortable and relaxed on its streets – this was where she had grown up: it was her home. Whenever she had to leave, however briefly, it was always a joy to return: she loved its sprawling outskirts, safe and clean, and its imposing centre – broad tree-lined boulevards, grand parks and ambitious new buildings on a scale that filled her heart with pride.

She had visited Shamura once, years ago. It was all dark corners and unpleasant surprises: squalor, chaos and dirt. The whole place was full of Light Elves, many from Karithia judging by their accents, squatting in ruined buildings and begging on the streets. The local authorities seemed content to let them simply loiter in packs, ready to attack and rob hapless passers-by or simply taunt and intimidate them for their own amusement. The whole place was a decrepit shadow of greatness: a warning of what could happen if complacency replaced vigilance and vigour.

But sometimes there were downsides to eternal

vigilance. Even now, she was almost certainly being watched. That was how things worked: that was the way she had made things work when she ran Internal Security.

But she was well aware of the Ministry's directives – she knew that no operative would board a small carriage or little boat with her and risk exposing their presence and identity: instead, they would either arrange alternative transport or, especially if her trip was not at all suspicious, simply wait for her to return. As such, Fort Na'Prar, half a mile offshore and now used only for short scenic visits by the residents of Pelledac, was an excellent location for a clandestine meeting.

An older couple dressed in heavy overcoats were the only other people on the twelve-seat ferry.

She disliked engaging in any furtive activity, especially so close to home, but she had private business that she hadn't managed to take care of in her previous role. Private business that she now must pursue using her own resources. And that meant taking calculated risks. If she was discovered, it would mean the end of her career. People would understand, of course: they would even excuse her, forgive her for being carried away by passion. Except that this wasn't passion at all: this was a considered decision and a long-term plan.

There was often a stiff breeze blowing in from the Kyllian Firth, so there were plenty of seats in sheltered locations around the fort. She found Ymal Zhulin sitting on a bench, tucked below the ruined north wall: the side that looked across the open waters.

She recognised him at once: she'd been worried that she might not.

Her parents had owned a cabin on Lake Pamor which they often visited during the summer months, to fish and relax: Zhulin had stayed just along the shore and they often ate and drank with him in the evenings. They didn't agree on most political or social matters but they put their differences aside, as people do when there's no-one else around.

One of the reasons she had learned how to access Ministry records for herself was to learn who they *didn't* have files on, so she was confident that no-one knew of any connection between her and Ymal Zhulin. She hadn't seen him since her mother's death. He hadn't even come to the memorial.

Hearing her approach, he looked up at her – at her scarred face – and then looked away.

'You weren't followed?' she checked as she sat down.

'Why would anyone follow me?' She didn't respond, and he eventually relented: 'I'm as sure as I can be. I took precautions, hopefully without being too obvious about it.'

'It's good to see you.'

'Because you have a use for me?'

'Not just that.'

'How's your father?'

'I haven't seen him for a long time.'

'You should.'

'He moved out to Teulen.'

'I heard that. But Teulen's not far.'

'I didn't ask you here for this,' she said, flatly.

'What, then?'

'I need someone to infiltrate the Free Brigade.' The Brigade were an extremist group that hated the Confederacy and its values: they sought to create chaos and disruption through intimidation and murder. They were sometimes known as Laktrists, even though Ivia Lakterr was surely long dead.

He snorted a laugh. 'Straight to the point, eh.'

'Straight to the point,' she agreed. 'I want to know if they ordered my mother's death.'

'You think they did?'

'Probably yes, but I haven't found any proof.'

'And you need to know for sure, so your soul can find some peace?'

'Peace? Founders!' she shook her head. 'Once I know for sure, I will tear them apart. I will find the people responsible and I will destroy them. Every last one of them. Them and their families and the people they love.'

Zhulin was silent for a few seconds. 'It was a long time ago,' he said eventually.

'Not to me.'

'So it seems. And why did you think of me for this? Why do you think I have the skills for this? Or the motivation?'

'I'm not stupid and I wasn't stupid then,' she told him. 'I knew about you and my mother.'

'I see.' He fell silent, and then commented: 'I was surprised when you went to work at the Ministry, but then I realised you were looking for whoever killed her. Most people thought it was the Secret Police.'

'It wasn't.'

'And you think it was Laktrists. Even if you're right, shouldn't the Ministry deal with them?'

'We've tried, me and all my predecessors, but they're stronger than other groups: their security's too tight. It's almost a standing joke in Internal Security, the number of times we've failed to place people in the Brigade. They operate with almost as much impunity as the East Wind.'

'Everyone thinks the East Wind is part of the government anyway.'

'They're not, but there's not much interest in stopping them. We have enough real enemies that we don't need to waste time on people who share our values. If anything, it's the other way round – it's the East Wind that's infiltrated the Ministry. There are plenty of people working there who support their goals *and* their methods: enough to pass on any information that might be useful to them.'

'I'd imagine that kind of extremism has a natural home at Internal Security,' Zhulin nodded. 'I'm surprised *you* left them alone, though. That's not like the Jetta I remember.'

'I'd have got round to them eventually, with a bit more time.'

'And the Free Brigade ...?'

'I have a name and a place, that's all,' she explained. 'But it should be enough.' She'd sat in on the interrogation that yielded the lead and she'd buried it deep in paperwork: put it aside for when she needed it.

He nodded: they both knew that he was going to do this. 'So how did you find me?' he asked.

'I've always known where you are. I saw when you put the cabin up for sale and moved here.' That had been four years ago.

'And no-one knows we're connected?'

'Not at the Ministry. And I can't think how the Free Brigade would find out. Here.' She passed him a small envelope that contained background information about the Brigade and their operations, details of her lead and the ways he could contact her safely. 'And you might need this.' She handed him a small purse.

'That's a lot,' he weighed it in his hand. 'Yours?'

'I don't have anything else to spend it on.'

'Your mother would have wanted you to move on with your life.'

'Yes, she would have. And that's exactly what I'll do when this is finished.' She stood up. 'I'll leave first.'

'I'll wait for a couple more hours. It's peaceful here: almost like Lake Pamor.'

On the ferry back, she wondered whether she should have told Zhulin that the Ministry had recently embedded their own operative in the Brigade. Probably not: the less he knew, the more convincing he would be. And the safer he would be. Besides, the Ministry's man would soon be compromised, if he hadn't already been.

Internal Security had successfully infiltrated the outermost cells of the Brigade several times over the past few years but as soon as anyone started making any real progress, they disappeared. She had her suspicions about why that might be.

Chapter Four

Friends and Partners

1

As the seasons turned from spring to summer and the days grew longer, he had dared hope that they might finally leave. Even Emindur, oppressive in the heat, would have been better than another month in the Hills. But there was no word.

This was a waste of everyone's time.

And despite his best efforts, the Emperor's health did not deteriorate – the damned priest was keeping him alive, of course, but he couldn't tell Hesketh that. The idiot lord was a fawning follower of the old religion and held Corvak in superstitious reverence.

The letter from Silvendor had shaken the old man, but had not weakened him. At first, the news of his brother's death left the Emperor a little more alert and engaged, a little more alive. He soon slipped back into the same lethargic disinterest as before and his grip on power remained unshaken.

It was a mystery how Silvendor knew.

How could *anyone* know?

The black lord had Eriskant killed far, far away. Far from anywhere, in a place where nobody knew him. That was what the black lord believed, that was what his thoughts betrayed: his glee at his own success.

But he had been wrong – someone had found out and had told Silvendor.

So not only does the black lord have enemies, but he makes mistakes.

What does it mean?

It doesn't matter what it means, Little Mouse. It will not change our plans.

The unofficial news of Eriskant's death had loosened tongues, and all kinds of rumours and stories rippled through the hill palaces.

Rumours about the Dead God's Crown, of course.

And the Tribute boy, and the big unnecessary war that he will cause.

And he heard voices talking of magefire at Q'ushar: magefire used in plain sight, against Elves.

How in the Three Lands had they let that happen? Who was stupid enough to risk the Truce? No-one wanted <u>*that*</u> *war surely: not now. Not even the black lord.*

Why would mages stand with the Confederacy?

There were conflicting stories, but Q'ushar was so very close to where the old man's brother had died.

It couldn't be a coincidence.

But nothing was clear.

2

The black shadow of the Keep behind Mironyx felt like some looming presence, impassively watching them.

'I'll catch you if you fall,' she told him.

He lay on his front and, achingly slowly, eased himself backwards over the edge of the palace roof until he was holding on to the stone gutter and his legs were dangling free, but he couldn't support his own weight and he fell. She tried her best to cushion his landing and they both collapsed to the ground. Neither of them cried out, so the soldiers wouldn't hear them.

He gathered up his toy bear Bakkuk from where she had dropped it and then they ran hand in hand into the darkness. She tried to drag him faster along with her but he pulled back – he was tired and confused and he couldn't have kept up with her anyway.

The palace gardens seemed to grow larger and larger as their pace slowed, curtained in every direction by high snow-covered peaks, the inescapable backdrop of Ruthin. Voices were shouting from all around the Keep behind them, and torches flickered in other parts of the grounds. There were screams: chilling, haunting screams of pain and fear that would live with her for years.

Miko had almost completely stopped.

She knew that she couldn't carry him, and if she stayed with him then she would die. So she crouched and looked into his confused tearful face, telling him: 'I will wait for you. At the lake. Beside the boats. But I can't wait for long. Run to the lake as fast as you can and I'll see you there.'

And then she let go of his hand and she ran.

Even without looking back, she knew that he wasn't following her: he was simply standing there in the middle of the path, alone in the night, holding Bakkuk. At that moment, he surely understood that she had not only abandoned him, but she had sacrificed him in order to save her own life.

Take your brother and run. That was what Nanny Etta had told her to do, and she had chosen not to.

She could still hear the echo of those words when she woke and it took her a moment to remember where she was. Her hand had instinctively reached for the knife under her pillow and she let her fingers rest on its reassuring cool metal handle for a few seconds. Then she stretched and breathed deeply.

Ruthin and the Keep had been continually on her mind for weeks now – months – and she had been dreaming of them far more frequently. At times, the dreams left her tired and irritable throughout the day, though hopefully she concealed it well enough that no-one noticed. Certainly no-one had commented. And if she made sounds in her sleep, no-one had commented on that either.

She had spent these long summer months travelling gradually north: day after tedious day on the road, punctuated by brief stops in small provincial capitals. From its beginning in Eastholm, this grand tour of the Western Steppes had been a furtive and unassuming affair: a long succession of unfamiliar rooms in unfamiliar inns and hostels. This was the dull, monotonous face of diplomacy and, as Aravan repeatedly assured her, was just as important to their plan as training and arming the men.

They had reached the remote kingdom of Irenthar, north of Falkenvey in the very corner of the Steppes. Beyond this point, beyond the Buckle Peaks to the north, lay the high plateau of Irlak. The White Mountains loomed to the west. From Irenthar they would turn south again, this time passing through Telleck and Imber before returning to Linnander where they would meet the others.

They chose not to wear the colours and symbols of Ruthin on the road. The Imperial presence in the wider Steppes was not as overt as it had been in earlier years –

their influence had declined following the war and they were no longer as welcome – but there would still be plenty of people happy to trade information for Imperial gold. In private, of course, they adopted all the trappings and uniforms of Ruthin; presented themselves as the legitimate government of Ruthin; presented her as the clear heir to the throne.

The General briefed her before each meeting: the discussions and communications that had already taken place, the approach that he judged best, and the outcomes they might hope for.

Almost exclusively, they met only the representatives of power – minor members of the royal families, diplomats, ministers of state, occasional officers in the military. And they had a slightly different approach prepared for each, words tailored not only to appeal to them but to those who stood behind them.

For the most part, Aravan explained, the lowly status of these contacts was simply to ensure that their discussions wouldn't attract any unwelcome attention. She didn't argue the point, but it seemed just as likely that they were an indication of how trivial and irrelevant their mission and their cause were regarded.

Before they even started, he had warned her that no-one would proclaim for them: not now, and not even when they took back the kingdom … they would be expected to quickly lose it again. So they would look foolish if they asked for that.

Instead they sought moral support; they stoked distrust and unease at the presence of the Empire; they smiled and tried to make friends for the future. Most importantly, they tried to reinforce the notion that everyone's interests would be best served if she was ruling her father's kingdom rather than the Empire, regardless how likely or unlikely that might seem. After each meeting, they left behind a small diplomatic mission: three or four people, to represent them in ongoing discussions and negotiations as the situation evolved.

'Every second of this is torture,' she complained to the General. 'You could find a hundred skilled diplomats and negotiators to take my place. This is not what I trained for.'

'On the contrary, my Lady, I think your training has been peculiarly appropriate. You project a detached ruthlessness which everyone interprets as proof that you are the royalty that you claim to be.' It was sometimes difficult to tell when the General was being entirely serious but she detected no hint of irony in his response. On several occasions she had noticed him struggling to contain his own instinct to lead in their discussions, so it seemed that he genuinely believed that she was better suited to it.

Here in Irenthar, their appointment was with the king's uncle, Prince Aygarth.

'You won't remember me, Princess,' he greeted her, 'but we've met before. On the occasion of your aunt's Majority, in Ravensgill.'

'I remember that day, Prince, but you're right,' she nodded: 'I was too young to pay any attention to the names and faces of our guests, however distinguished.'

'And we entertained your royal father here on more than one occasion. He was a frequent visitor to the courts of the region, easing tensions and cementing alliances: for all that he was arrogant, he knew the value of his neighbours. And he understood that diplomacy comes from a position of mutual advantage: each side offers something that will benefit the other.' Atterlie smiled, knowing the question that would come. 'What is it that you offer us now? You and your war?'

'We offer you a better future,' she told him. 'A future without Imperial troops camped on your doorstep, interfering and intimidating …'

They had rehearsed the questions and answers, honed and sharpened them as her mission had progressed. Her challenge now was not deciding what to say, but in presenting her answers as if they were spontaneous.

'That was one of our best meetings,' General Aravan told her as they left the tiny rural palace, little more than a glorified hunting lodge.

'Just as pointless as all the others,' she disagreed wearily. 'Just as pointless as this whole trip. As Falkenvey and Flax and all the other little kingdoms.'

'We started this journey with no friends and little hope of finding any, my lady. We end it with a network of people who know your face and know that the cause of Ruthin is not extinct.'

'But not one soldier or one gold Crown committed to our cause.'

'Neither of us believed we would reach the end of this with bulging coffers and an army of liberation at our backs. We have accomplished what we intended to accomplish.'

'You're right,' she sighed, 'but I wish we had more to rely on than the weak and the fearful.'

'As do I, my lady, but all we have is ourselves and our allies among the rebels.'

'Is there really no-one else within Ruthin? What happened to the aristocracy? The Clans?'

'Half the aristocrats fled as soon as Ravensgill fell, forfeiting their lands and their assets to Struving's friends and allies. Those who stayed pledged loyalty to the new rulers, so it's difficult to imagine them supporting us. And as for the Clans, we're in contact with the First of Dog in Ruthin, but they won't help: not as a Clan.'

Across the Three Lands, Light Elves were organised according to Nine Clans, creating a parallel structure of loyalty and power that crossed borders and was founded on family rather than politics. Dog Clan was the clan of fighters and warriors and would have been the most useful to support their cause.

'Can we change that?' she asked.

'Unfortunately there are many who see advantages in the occupation: Dog clan has always prospered under Imperial rule. So their First chooses to remain neutral.'

'And the First of Nine?' The First of Nine acted as a moderator in disputes or differences of opinion among the Nine Clans.

'Approaching her would be risky, since we don't know where her sympathies lie. And besides, she wouldn't go against the First of Dog. Not on a Clan matter.'

'So we're left begging favours from our hesitant and nervous neighbours.'

'You can't blame them. We are an unknown, a gamble: they assume that we will fail, so they won't commit to anything that they might regret later. The Empire would be a powerful enemy. But we've prepared the ground, and that's what we set out to do. Now, they will wait and watch what happens. It's the mission of those we leave behind to persuade them that there will be a moment – a set of circumstances or a situation on the ground – when it will be not only acceptable but advisable to declare for us and to offer practical support. Men and arms, if they are required.'

'We seem a long way from that point,' she smiled, tired of this conversation and the dozens of similar discussions that they'd had over the past few weeks.

'If they believe for just a moment that we can hold Ruthin and keep the Empire from their doors, then we can persuade them. And your presence here makes that seem more likely,' he reassured her.

'It would be useful to have at least some idea how many of them will actually support us.'

'Yes, it would,' he agreed, 'but we do not have that luxury. I believe they will act as one, though: when the moment comes, they will decide together what to do. Unfortunately, we can't tell which voices will speak most strongly in our favour and which will be against us. No matter what any of them say, their true intentions will only be revealed when they act.'

'Perhaps we should take the Confederacy's help after all,' she said, though not seriously. 'It would be more straightforward than all of this.'

'That would still be possible, my lady: this is politics. Everyone understands that no position is ever absolute.'

She didn't want to have that conversation either. 'I will be happy when we are done with all this diplomacy.'

'As will I, my lady. As will I. But now we must ride south to Telleck, and discover what our messengers have arranged with King Uhrpan and his representatives. And then Imber.'

'And after that, Ruthin.'

'We have more preparations to make and our forces must be readied but after that, yes. Ruthin.'

She would never admit it to the General, but the idea of simply setting foot in Ruthin made her feel more than a little nervous. Perhaps it was because she'd never returned, never gone home: her last memories of her own kingdom were of crossing the border south into Belsace, wearing badly-fitting clothes and with her hair cut short.

It wasn't clear even to her why she had avoided Ruthin so completely these last thirteen years – she could easily have passed through last year, when she had a contract in Falkenvey, but she had preferred to keep to the Steppes. She told herself that it would be too dangerous, though she knew that there was very little risk: no-one in Ruthin would recognise her. Even Aravan had not recognised her.

Nonetheless she had felt uncomfortable with the idea. And still did.

3

The little hall, surely more familiar with social celebrations and receptions, was equally well suited to hosting a clandestine council of war. Ensuring that there were no unwelcome interruptions, the doors were guarded by a number of Captain Redwolf's soldiers and fighters from Ruthin. Inside, almost fifty people had gathered, gradually arriving in ones and twos.

A number of the Company were sitting on the edge of a small stage.

'Well?' Magda asked Lanvik.

'I don't think I've ever seen a group that looked more ill at ease,' he admitted. 'The Captain's people look like soldiers, but the fighters from Ruthin are more like bandits. I suppose we look like thugs and killers and Foxblade looks as if she's never been around other people before. Everyone's trying their best to appear casual and looking even more suspicious because of it.'

'As suspicious as that horn case you carry around?'

'Perhaps not *that* suspicious,' he agreed with a smile.

The hall was on the outskirts of Stannet in Linnander, on the western branch of the Great River perhaps two hundred miles east of Ruthin. As well as the Company, there were around twenty of Captain Redwolf's people. A further two dozen resistance fighters from Ruthin represented various groups and factions: when Foxblade entered the room, they had all followed her with their eyes but said nothing.

'We should begin,' the Captain suggested. He had pulled two tables together in the centre of the room, to accommodate a large map of Ruthin.

'Who are they?' one the resistance fighters indicated Slorn, who had positioned himself close to the table.

'He is a mercenary, and these are some of his people. They're here at the Queen's bidding, not mine, but we've worked together before and I can vouch for them. They're trustworthy. Honourable.'

'I don't know if we need "honourable",' the man sounded hostile.

'We can be as dishonourable as we need to be,' Slorn shrugged.

'Let's not start by bickering,' Redwolf said.

'No,' Slorn agreed. 'We're all here to listen to your plan. Particularly how you intend using your two frigates.' Mountainous Ruthin was about as far from the sea as was possible in the whole Three Lands.

'We have a lot more resources than those ships. We have horses, artillery and wagons, cannon, munitions and trained troops already on the way north to Cerinium. You can hide an army in Cerinium if you know the right people.'

'And when will this army of yours march on Ruthin?' one of the resistance leaders asked.

'It's not possible to march on Ruthin. Moving any large force much further north risks detection: there are roadblocks and spies, and the lands around Ruthin are full of Imperial troops. Word would have reached Ravensgill and probably the Empire by the time we crossed the border.'

'So how will you take back the kingdom without your army?'

'We'll use a smaller force to take control of communications across Ruthin, at night and in secret, before bringing in the rest of our forces. If Struving's men don't know what's happening, they won't leave their barracks.' He leaned over the table and began to point out critical routes, checkpoints and roadblocks, guardposts and fortifications, in each case explaining their significance and how they could be neutralised. Comments and questions from the others developed into a detailed tactical analysis of places that Lanvik had never heard of and had no chance of ever remembering. Together with most of the Company, he quickly became bored and disengaged. Slorn and Bane remained at the table with Foxblade.

It took more than an hour before one of the rebel leaders asked: 'How many troops will it take you to do this?'

'A few hundred would give us the best chance of succeeding, but we can't slip that many across the border unnoticed and then keep them hidden, waiting. So we'll do it with around ninety, mostly Aldarian Guard, divided into six groups of fifteen.' One of the resistance men laughed, but the Captain continued: 'They will be supported by another hundred already in Ruthin, who are not fighters.'

'Do they know about this plan?'

'Not yet.'

'Ninety's a joke,' someone else said, brutally.

'It'll be difficult, yes, and that's why we need your help. You represent the three largest groups fighting in Ruthin: hundreds of fighters.'

'And we've kept those hundreds of fighters alive by not staging anything like this. This would risk everything.'

'So what's your alternative? After all these years, you are still alive but the Empire is no closer to leaving Ruthin than it was on the day its legions marched in.'

'We haven't received as much help as we needed.' That sounded like an accusation.

'I helped as much as I could, with money and people, but it didn't accomplish anything. People died, but nothing changed. That's why I've been preparing my own people for this instead.'

It looked as if the discussion might continue for some time and with increasing rancour, but Foxblade suddenly spoke, picking a brief lull so that her voice caught everyone's attention. 'We are all on the same side here. Let us not do the Empire's work for them.'

No-one spoke, waiting for her to say more.

'Even if we could field a hundred thousand, we couldn't defeat the Empire in open combat,' she told them. 'And everything we've done to disrupt their occupation so far has achieved little more than destroy our own land. At most, we're an irritation. The General's plan may not be perfect and it certainly doesn't offer any guarantee of success, but what other options do we have? I wouldn't be here if I didn't believe that this is our best hope. Perhaps our only hope.'

Regardless of how many people agreed with her, she'd stopped the argument and diffused the tension in the room.

'So what do you want from us?' one of the resistance leaders said eventually.

'There are a number of soft targets that need watched in case they cause difficulties,' Redwolf explained. 'The Watch, local administration in Ravensgill and the larger towns, some border posts and road-blocks, individual guards and security, a few night-time patrols. More than that, if any of Struving's units get wind of trouble, we'll need your help to manage them until the rest of our army reaches Ruthin.'

'What else?' the man asked.

'You have to stop any messages from reaching the Empire's forces at the Gate. To succeed, we need to close and hold the Gate: we won't be able to do that if they mobilise.'

'A few dozen men can deal with the beacons, but the Highway is a different matter. In your father's day, the message was carried by a single runner,' the man nodded slightly towards Foxblade. 'Now they use a company of armed men, or a half company. It takes longer, but it's a lot more secure. They learned from our mistakes.'

'We can't engage professional soldiers in those numbers,' another of the resistance fighters added. 'We'll be cut to pieces.'

'I can't spare any men to help you, but you won't be alone.' Redwolf looked across. 'The Human will be with you.' He indicated Lanvik.

'One Human?'

'He has useful and particular skills,' Foxblade spoke up. 'You will succeed with his help.'

The last time she had spoken no-one challenged her, but now one of the resistance leaders asked, 'You're sure?'

'I'm certain.'

She sounded much more confident than Lanvik felt.

She had only told him what she wanted last week. 'You said you'd do whatever I need,' she said, 'and this is what I need. And it's better if you're there: if anyone can find a way to avoid a lot of unnecessary deaths, it's you.'

'What about your army?' the discussion continued.

'They'll cross the border from Belsace in the early hours and should be in Ravensgill by dawn. They'll engage any of Struving's forces that take the field, in pitched battles and sieges, and should reach the Gate by midday.'

'What about the west?' With the Gate closed, the western part of Ruthin would be cut off.

'We'll have to surrender the west for a time. But that's always been Ruthin's philosophy, to give up half the country until our allies arrive.'

'And what allies would those be?'

'Our traditional allies will come, but not at once,' Redwolf said, clearly. 'They do not trust that we have the will or the resources to do this; they do not trust that the people will be with us; and they do not trust that we won't bicker and fight amongst ourselves. So they would be fools to set themselves against the Empire until we prove ourselves.'

'How do we do that? Prove ourselves?'

'Most likely by holding the kingdom for six months.'

'Six months? But the Empire will be upon us in weeks!'

One of the other resistance fighters spoke up: 'And they'll be more vicious than before, to anyone who stands against them.'

'What of the people?' Slorn spoke for the first time. 'Will they rise up and fight with you? Or will they stand against you?'

'Why would they stand against us?'

'There must be thousands who've thrown their lot in with Struving and his family, whose livelihoods depend on them. And a whole generation has reached adulthood under the occupation. Like it or not, there will be at least some who support the Empire.'

'The whole population will prefer peace to an ongoing war,' the Captain assured him.

'Of course they will, but some will believe that the best path to a peace and prosperity lies within the Empire. To them, you are the ones starting this war, or at least perpetuating it.'

'Some people will think like that, yes,' one of the Ruthin fighters admitted. 'But less, now that the rightful Queen stands with us.'

'I'm not Queen yet,' Foxblade reminded them.

'It doesn't matter how much of the population is with us or against us,' another voice insisted. 'We still cannot hold Ruthin for six months against the Empire.'

'We will make our move three weeks after the equinox,' the Captain said, 'when the first snows have reached Ruthin but the deep cold has not closed in. Even the Empire cannot launch a winter campaign in the mountains.'

'And what of you?' the most vocal of the resistance leaders turned to Slorn. 'What is your part in this?'

'Our task will be to take the Keep.'

The man laughed. 'It's not possible to "take" the Keep. Like the Iron Gate, a tiny number can defend it against an army.'

Slorn shrugged. 'And exactly like the Gate, it will fall if people do not know if it is being attacked.'

'And how will you achieve that?'

'That's my concern. I am not part of General Aravan's plan or your alliance: my services were secured directly by Princess Vy'Rhienn.'

'It is important to take the Keep and Duke Struving,' Foxblade spoke up. 'Not as important as the Gate, but still important. If he is not removed then the Empire will have an excuse to send a force to relieve him – he would become a symbol to rally our enemies. And if we take the Keep, it will be a signal to the people that Ruthin is truly free.'

'So what will we do with him and his family?'

'I'd prefer not to execute them in cold blood, but circumstances might demand that.' She shrugged, easily: everyone in the room would know what had happened to her family.

'And where will you be, my Lady? While these events unfold?'

'The Princess will be in Ruthin,' Redwolf explained, 'but safely hidden until we have control. We can't risk anything happening to her.'

Their discussions seemed to be drawing to a close, but one of the resistance leaders – a Dark Elf – said, 'You haven't mentioned the four legions stationed east of the Gate. Even the Iron Gate is no defence if you have enemies on both sides.'

'You're right – once we've taken the kingdom, they are the biggest threat. But their own situation will be precarious – without access to the Gate, they lose communication and co-ordination with Imperial forces to the west. They'll have problems establishing new supply chains as winter begins to close in, since they haven't made many friends locally. And although many of their troops are campaign-hardened, they'll also be weary and carrying injuries and losses.'

'All of that is true, but they'll still number at least fifteen thousand soldiers. We can't take them on in any fight.'

'No, we can't. But if we engage with the individual commanders, I'm sure we can reach some accommodation. They'll be isolated and exposed so they'll be looking for an excuse to retreat, to march south and over the border to Biravia.'

'You think they'll just leave?'

'If their commanders are rational men, then yes. But we'll fight if we have to.'

There were discussions on trivial and administrative questions after that, but the meeting was essentially done. The parties agreed how they would contact each other during the coming weeks, and ended with a toast to Princess Vy'Rhienn and a free Ruthin. Then they spun off into small, more private conversations.

One of the Terevarna fighters from Ruthin – they were mostly Terevarna – walked over to the Company. 'If we agree to guard the Highway, then we may be fighting alongside you,' he addressed Lanvik bluntly.

'Yes. My name's Lanvik.' There had been no names given during the meeting, and Lanvik assumed that such groups preferred not to share their real identities.

The man introduced himself, 'I'm Hurr, Dinian Hurr.' Then, as if to belie Lanvik's assumption, he pointed out the two others who had done most of the talking: 'That is Savvat of Vissdale and the Dark Elf is Captain Hodier. We are only Elves here, but there are Humans who fight with us.'

'Not so many?'

'No. Not because they are lacking in bravery or loyalty, but because there are not so many Humans in Ruthin. Perhaps the weather is too harsh for them.'

'Perhaps they just haven't learned to dress for it,' Lanvik suggested.

The man laughed and then casually asked, 'Do you also believe that you can help us overcome half a company of Imperial troops?'

'Yes,' Lanvik said, simply. He resisted the urge to glance towards the long case that held his staff, lying beside the stage.

Hurr waited a few seconds for any explanation or additional detail and then said, 'Your colleague was equally reticent about how he plans to take the Keep …'

'That's understandable, especially if he plans some subterfuge.' Slorn had discussed the matter with the rest of the Company a few days before. They would be entering Ruthin as performers, and he no doubt already had ideas about how to gain access to Struving's ruling circle and therefore the Keep itself. Lanvik would cross the border separately and not associate with the others. That would be safer.

Once Dinian Hurr had returned to his colleagues, Lanvik commented, 'I'm still surprised that Kiergard agreed to all of this, even for the money.'

'I think that's more to do with Elisha of Giren Pass than any noble principles. Or even the fee,' Tremano suggested.

'You're right,' Magda agreed. 'I think he's worried about what might happen to her.'

'I expected her to be here,' Lanvik said.

'She's already in Ruthin.' It seemed that Magda was privy to more information than the others. 'The Captain keeps some of his people there all the time, which means they have places that are safe and people they trust.'

'He uses women, mainly,' Foxblade joined them. 'In Ruthin and among the refugees.' Lanvik had noticed that the rest of the Company treated her almost as an honorary member. They trusted her enough not to become guarded when she came within earshot, as they did with everyone else. 'They gather information, but also spread rumours and stir up discontent. To undermine confidence. It's another form for fighting.'

'Talking?' Tyrell was unconvinced.

'Words can be a very effective weapon,' Menska told him. 'They're like poison. And they can be fast-acting or slow-acting depending how you craft them.'

'And he probably uses women because he wants it done properly,' Magda joked.

'They're better at it, just as the men are better at pretending to be pirates,' Foxblade answered seriously. 'Read into that what you will, but don't dismiss it as easier work. It's dangerous, and he loses a number of people every year.' She turned to Lanvik and touched his arm: 'I'll see you afterwards, but I have to mingle now.'

'I understand,' he nodded. 'Go and be diplomatic.'

As she walked away, Magda quietly asked: 'And you're committed to stop a unit of trained Imperial Troops for her?'

'If I have to, yes.' He felt he had to explain, 'I owe her.'

'That's a big favour.' The rest of the Company were familiar with his thoughts about violence.

'Yes,' he nodded. 'Yes, it is. But I'll try to avoid killing anyone.'

He hoped that he sounded a lot more confident than he felt. Realistically, if there *was* a confrontation with Imperial soldiers then he could demonstrate his power and warn them to turn back or surrender. But he wondered what he would actually do if they forced his hand …

He hadn't told any of the others that he had agreed to more than that.

If Imperial forces mobilised despite their efforts, Foxblade had asked him to hold the Iron Gate alone until Redwolf's army arrived.

4

The Company had taken three rooms in a small inn that mainly catered to itinerant traders. It sported a large and comfortable bar, converted from a stable, in which it offered simple local meals as well as drinks.

Slorn gathered Magda, Bane, Garran, Tyrell and Vorrigan together in one of the rooms, while the others were drinking downstairs.

'I have a plan for those legions east of the Gap,' he told them.

'Something you don't want to share with the Captain's people,' Magda observed. 'Or the others.'

'In that case, I must be here because you need my particular talents,' Vorrigan guessed. 'Do you want me to sell something? Or forge something?'

Slorn smiled slightly and admitted, 'I need you to make up some sealing wax, with a very particular appearance.'

Vorrigan thought for a moment and then asked: 'Like one of the Private Imperial Codes?'

'That's right.' *How do you even know about those? This is what I get when I surround myself with criminals*, he reminded himself.

'Do you have a sample?'

'No.'

'It doesn't matter how old it is,' Vorrigan assured him. 'Or how much you have. But I'm going to have to see some.'

'I can describe it accurately.'

'You think your memory's good enough?'

'I haven't seen it for a while, but neither have the people it's for. They won't look at it too long or too carefully, so it has to be a good match but it doesn't have to be perfect. It's a dark bluish-red, flecked with purple and black.'

'I don't know that one.'

'It's not used very often.'

'I'll be able to get what I need in Stannet, so I'll make up a some samples tomorrow and we can work on them together until we get it right. Won't you need a seal?'

'I already have one,' he said, without sharing any details. 'But I'll need some paper as well. Standard Imperial Court.'

'That could be trickier than the wax. And easier to spot if we get it wrong. It needs the right absorbency, brightness, weight, transparency and consistency,' Vorrigan counted off the words on his fingers. 'How much do you need?'

'Half a dozen sheets at least.'

'I wish you'd asked at the Lodge: I've got all kinds of supplies there. Or even in Cerinium. When do you need it?'

'As soon as possible.'

'It's always "as soon as possible" …'

'When we're done, there will be four letters that need hand-delivered, one to each of the legionary Commanders east of the Gap,' Slorn continued.

'And we're to be your messengers,' Garran nodded. 'Me and Tyrell.'

'You have the right accents. And Imperial training.'

'So do you,' Garran said. 'And Bane.'

'Yes, but there's a risk we'd be recognised,' Slorn told him.

'By a random Commander in the field? Just how high profile was your escapade at Court, whatever it was?'

'Not that high,' Slorn forced a smile. 'But I'd rather not roll against Dark Aoshay.' The God of puzzles, shapes and treachery was also the God of luck, both good and bad.

Luck, though, didn't really enter into the matter. He assumed that at least half the legionary Commanders would recognise him immediately, considering how many formal parades, audiences and councils he had attended. Bane wouldn't be so widely known by sight but he had a reputation in certain circles because of his size.

'So we'll need two Imperial uniforms,' he added. 'And travel documents to go with them.'

'You want me to sort the uniforms?' Magda asked.

'You and Bane, yes,' he confirmed, 'and Vorrigan, if he can help. And anyone else you need.'

'What can we tell the others?'

'Whatever you choose.' He trusted her judgement.

'How do two messengers deliver four letters?' Tyrell asked.

'Two legions each,' Slorn said. 'They're all quartered reasonably close to each other – two or three days ride, at most.'

'Won't they be suspicious if we rush straight off?'

'No. They won't expect you to wait for a reply: each legion will have its own people for carrying messages. And if they suggest that you stay, you can explain that you have another letter to deliver.'

Magda waited behind after the others left.

'You don't need my help,' she said. 'Why was I here?'

'I wanted you to know about this.'

'You didn't ask my opinion, so you'd already decided.'

'And?'

'I've never seen you like this before, so … involved,' she told him. 'It's as if you're possessed or on some religious quest, so the normal rules of sense and profit and risk don't apply. I don't understand why you would go to these lengths for Ruthin. Or even for Elisha.'

'Mm,' he said, regretting that he had asked her.

He had tried not to think too deeply about his motivation, because he already knew that his actions didn't make sense: if he actually confronted that fact then he might talk himself out of what he was doing, and he didn't want that. The more he could do for Elisha, the more he could fight *her* battles, surely the more likely it would be that she survived.

'And I don't understand how your plan is going to work anyway. What message could you possibly send that would influence the actions of an Imperial legion?' she frowned at him. Despite the scarring on her face and her half-shut eye, he recognised her penetrating expression.

'I still have to work that out,' Slorn told her with a smile.

'Well, we both know *that's* a lie,' she said, holding his gaze. Then she stood and left the room.

She was right, of course. He knew exactly what he was going to write.

He would create a simple message that included a number of innocuous but infrequently used words: words that formed part of a particular code, created to allow the Imperial Family to communicate directly and securely with senior Commanders. The code was a form of insurance. In the event that any faction turned against the Imperial Family – perhaps the Court or the High Command – the legions and fleets could be deployed directly. Most importantly, and most usefully in this circumstance, they would follow his instructions without communicating or seeking to confirm the order through the normal chain of command.

There was a specific wax to be used, which Vorrigan would create, and he would seal the letters with a genuine signet ring inscribed with the Pevensal Seal of the Military High Command. The message inside would instruct those legions to return to Emindur. Immediately.

But there would be a cost.

This was knowledge that could only be used once. The codes would be changed as soon as his deception was uncovered, so he was discarding one of the few weapons that he could have used against his own family: against Silvendor. At the very least, these codes might have bought him some time.

Using the codes and the seal would also significantly increase the likelihood that people believed he was still alive.

There were only two rings bearing the seal that were unaccounted for at Court: his and his uncle's, assuming that no-one had recovered Eriskant's ring from Haadar. Either ring could have been used by anyone, of course, but using one in conjunction with the codes made it far more likely that he was responsible. Senior members of the Court would reason that the Emperor's youngest son must be to blame, even if there was no clear motive. And supporting Ruthin against the Empire would surely damage his future chances of becoming Emperor, whether the letters were successful or not.

Of course, the codes might already have been changed, in which case he was sending Garran and Tyrell to their deaths; which was unfortunate but unavoidable.

At least he wouldn't have to wait very long to find out.

By the time his letters were being acted upon, one way or the other, the Company should be in Ruthin. They should see the results for themselves.

Chapter Five

Against the Dark

1

When Pireon asked Dach and Dasha about their father's study, they both remembered playing there. They would hide inside with the door closed and listen to people in the library: the thrill had come from being unobserved, rather than from anything they actually overheard. He discovered that the little room, of which he had been completely ignorant, had been one of their special places.

Neither of them remembered ever being in the room when their father was working, though: in their memories, the desk was always clear of books and papers.

He didn't mention to either of them how their father's last message had led him to the study. And he didn't mention how the little room had been searched … by their uncle, he assumed.

I don't trust them with this, he realised. *I don't trust Dach not to take this and use it somehow. And I don't trust either of them to keep it secret from Quiron.* Dach had never been close to their uncle but now that Quiron and Dasha were pair-bonded, their relationship was more complex.

The puzzle occupied him for days after his discovery, and then intermittently through the weeks that followed.

Why would his father create a secret message to reveal the presence of a room that everyone already knew about, even his own children? If he had left something precious there, then he must have known that anyone could simply take it.

Eventually, the matter drifted to the back of his mind. His days were simply too busy to remain focussed on a problem that yielded no clues and no progress. Juggling the routine of his classes and duties with his relationship meant that his only idle time was while walking the long path between the Seminary and the Oracle, and he normally devoted that time to mulling over the puzzles and paradoxes that the Hierarch presented him with during their private lessons.

Despite his lack of free time, or perhaps because of it, the hot summer months felt glorious that year. There were no pilgrimages, no missions for the Gods and no journeys beyond Elagion: instead, the entire summer seemed like one impossibly long day that he was able to spend with Iera. Even as he lived it, he knew that this would be the happiest time of his life, bettering even his half-imagined childhood on Kayoden. There was nothing about it that could have been improved. When he prayed in the Mother Temple or when he detoured to stand quietly in the Circle for a few moments, he offered thanks to all the Gods for this life that they had given him.

As they grew together, his relationship with Iera evolved into something more comfortable and less frantic. It wasn't that their passion had faded, only that it had matured: deepened. He half-expected them to become intimate over that summer – he couldn't think of it in any terms more explicit than "*becoming intimate*" – but they didn't. That would happen when it happened.

Almost before he knew it, the summer had passed and the Festival of Heart and Home and Soil was upon them again.

'What are you doing for Homeday?' he asked Dach.

'We'll spend it on Irriandor. Kayoden next year.'

'I used to think you didn't go back for Homeday because you were avoiding Dasha,' Pireon admitted. 'I thought it was horrible of you.'

'I wasn't avoiding Dasha, silly boy. I was avoiding Quiron. He always seemed to be telling me what to do. What about you? Are you going back, or will you spend it here?' He meant with Iera on Elagion.

'I think I'll go to Kayoden.'

'Haven't you seen enough of the place for one year?' Dach laughed.

He had a good point – Pireon had spent several days on the family estate over the last year, including the previous Homeday. That stood in dramatic contrast to the preceding five years, when he hadn't visited at all. He was beginning to feel comfortable there – it might not be his home, but it no longer felt like a strange and alien place. It didn't feel haunted by the ghosts of his parents any more, which was surely because he had become closer to the rest of his family.

As well as Dasha, he was looking forward to seeing Amphet and Ilada and their children; and even his Aunt Uthraiche, who had terrified him when he was little.

He took one of Elagion's boats, packed with excited priests and neophytes, as far as Aistolea. An even busier public ferry carried him across to the dam: as usual, it was as if all of Corvak was on the move. At the Elevator, he stood right at the very edge, braced against the rush of wind that permanently buffeted the face of the dam, and watched as the waters of Lake Olchos seemed to rise up to meet them as the giant locks drained.

The estate had no other visitors for Homeday and he was assigned one of the smaller first floor guest rooms in the new wing, rather than being banished to the attic as usual. Vialta hadn't laid out any clothes for him other than a pair of socks which she left on his bed and which might have been intended as an ironic joke.

He arrived early in the afternoon, several hours before dinner, and found Amphet, Ilada and Dasha on the terrace overlooking the lake. Quiron was engaged with family business, and Uthraiche was presumably busy with whatever normally kept her occupied. The three children were playing nearby, only occasionally in view but always audible.

'You didn't bring your girl from the Oracle?' Ilada asked.

'No, I didn't. She can't really leave Elagion.'

'How's that going to work out?' Dasha asked. 'If she can't leave Elagion?'

'Work out?' he repeated, a little testily. He wondered if it had been a subject of family discussion.

'I'm sorry,' Dasha shook her head. 'That was clumsy. What I meant was, have you thought what's going to happen in the future? Between the two of you. When you leave Elagion.'

'*If* I leave Elagion,' he said. 'I might stay.'

'Gods, well let's hope that doesn't happen,' Dasha laughed. 'After last year, we're all expecting you to graduate spectacularly and get a good posting. Imagine if you kept failing and were stuck there forever!'

That wasn't what he'd meant.

It was a long way in the future, but recently he'd been mulling over the idea of applying for a posting on Elagion itself when the time came. Most Junior Priests gained the experience they needed in the Temples of the Floating Cities and beyond, but a small number never left.

Ilada forcefully changed the topic, as if feeling guilty for raising it in the first place, and they discussed how warm and fine the summer had been.

That evening they ate in the main dining room, gathered around a single table to recite the Homeday prayer:

Whatever we treasure, that is our Heart.
Wherever our children sleep, that is our Home.
Wherever we stand, that is our Soil.

There were alternatives to the traditional Homeday meal available, but Pireon filled his plate with mingettes and ramagar, and a couple of spoons of sour dellenberries.

They certainly weren't among his favourites, but they were seldom available at any other time of the year. The act of eating them was somehow appropriate regardless whether he actually liked them, like the prayers that might accompany some tedious annual sacrament. This year, he drank Luvian wine with his meal. After his travels, he would surely have a higher tolerance to alcohol than before, but he still drank only moderately. There would be plenty later, if he wanted.

As they ate, he was involved in all the conversations around the table, rather than being sidelined as he had been on his first visit. Everyone else might be treating him differently, of course, but he felt that the change was mostly within himself: he was no longer afraid of simply joining in and offering his own opinions.

After eating, the adults stayed at the table for more than an hour before moving to the terrace. The children ran round and round the main house, laughing and shouting under the watchful attention of the servants.

There was a distinct chill in the evening air, a foretaste of the colder months ahead. They all remarked on it and drew their clothes tighter about them, eventually making their excuses shortly after sunset and retiring back inside.

Before going to bed, Pireon walked through to the library and operated the hidden catch to open the study door: the room was still his father's study, in his mind, even though it held no trace of him. He let the door close behind him, so that there was almost no light from the dim night-lamp in the library and the room was bathed in Hindera's cool blue light through the window instead. He ran his fingers across the top of the desk and then stood for a few minutes simply staring out at the gardens before heading up to his room for the night.

The damage to the chair and the desk irked him. He couldn't think of anywhere else in the house where furniture would be left in such a state, even if it wasn't immediately visible. The basic training he had received on Elagion was not sufficient for him to make professional repairs but the staff would surely have the skills, or else they would know appropriate tradesmen. He was still reluctant to mention it, though: word would get back to Quiron, directly or indirectly, and he didn't want his Uncle to know that anyone had noticed. Not until he was ready to talk about it: not until he knew what questions he wanted to ask.

He came down for breakfast a little after dawn the next morning and found Quiron already there. It seemed to be a family custom to rise late during holidays but his uncle had some business matters to attend to. Pireon remarked that he hadn't thought anyone would be trading on the middle day of the Homeday Festival.

'Not that kind of business,' Quiron said. 'Personal business. Family business, with friends and colleagues. Tedious stuff, but I know I can find them at home today.' He left early on one of the family launches, accompanied by two of the staff.

Pireon returned to the library. After a few minutes searching among the shelves dedicated to Kiritas family history and its estate, he found a volume that concerned the "new wing" – the southern extension to the original house.

He laid the book flat on one of the library's two broad tables, and leafed through the pages of preliminary discussions, requirements and estimates as well as the story of the works themselves. Eventually, he found a detailed plan of the ground floor and was able to trace the internal walls with one finger. In this document, all six windows opened onto the single large room. There was no discrepancy, no hidden door and no secret room: the library extended all the way to the south stair.

He wondered if the study had been deliberately omitted from the plans, to better preserve its secret. Or perhaps it had been a late change during construction, after the plans had been drawn up. He supposed the partition might even have been added at some later time: the new wing had been standing for four hundred years, which was plenty of time for modifications.

He could hear the sound of the children laughing somewhere in the grounds, though they weren't anywhere in sight through the windows, so Amphet and Ilada must be awake. Like everyone else, the children hadn't seemed at all surprised to see him here. It was perhaps because of that familiarity that he felt no pressure to fit in or act like anyone other than his usual self. He even felt relaxed around Quiron and Uthraiche, certainly compared with his visit last Homeday.

He turned over the remaining pages, one by one. The book ended with a series of particularly fine engravings: detailed elevations of the entire building. The exterior of the original east and west wings had been restyled during construction to give the house a single unified appearance, and the engravings showed the architect's intent. The building in the pictures resembled the house he was familiar with, but perfect, clean and unblemished: an ideal.

It was ironic but probably typical that the book focussed on what was new, what they were creating, even though he and anyone else who might read the volume in the future would already be familiar with this version of the house. It would have been far more interesting to see what had been there *before* the extension.

Of course, somewhere in the Library there might be another, older volume detailing the construction of the original house.

He turned to the image of the library windows that his father had pointed him towards: windows in the shape of the teardrops of Humans. They had been described in poetry as the *Tears of Ardendar*, or so Dasha had told him. He still hadn't read the poem.

He ran his fingers over them and over the little decorative roundels above them.

Gods, there aren't six windows at all. There are twelve windows.

Each large window had a smaller circular window above it for decorative balance, he supposed, or simply to provide more light. The redwether flower design might have been an excellent artistic choice, but windows that were so narrow at the top wouldn't effectively light any room with high ceilings.

He glanced up at the roundels and then walked into his father's study, where there was only one window. There was a missing window: *another* missing window.

It had been obvious from the first that the little room had a much lower ceiling than the library, but he'd assumed that difference was to accommodate the landing halfway up the south stairs. Perhaps the sixth round window actually looked onto that landing and he'd simply never noticed it.

He flicked through the pages of the open book, but the floorplans didn't show any overlap between the library and the stairs. Even so, he walked round to the stairs and then up to the landing. Just as he had remembered, wide picture windows let light into the hall below. It was clear that the entire stairwell lay beyond the library windows. He investigated the space beneath the landing and discovered that it was occupied by storage and a small side door, not by his father's study.

'I'm afraid it's locked,' one of the servants told him as he tried the handle. 'Is there anything I can help you with?'

'No. Thank you.'

He returned to the study and stared up at the ceiling: half-concealed among the decorative mouldings was a small metal loop that looked like a disused lamp fitting.

He had noticed a long wooden pole resting in the window alcove, with a double-ended hook at the end, and had assumed that it was for opening or closing the window or perhaps the curtain. He took the pole in both hands and reached up with it: the length was perfect to snare the little loop, though it took him a couple of attempts. He pulled and a hatch in the ceiling opened downwards by a couple of inches: its edges had been cut to fit the pattern of the moulding, making it all but invisible when closed.

It seemed that there *was* a secret room after all, hidden right above the study, and the only way to know it was there was to count the windows.

How in the Three Lands had he missed this the first time?

He mentally apologised to his father for being so slow and stupid.

He locked the study door from inside and drew the curtain at the window – he didn't want to risk being seen – and then he pulled the pole slowly downwards. The hatch swung fully open and a rope ladder tumbled down: he steadied it and climbed up, his heart pounding, wishing that he'd thought to bring a lamp with him. He was too excited to fetch one now: too excited to delay. When he reached the hatch, of course, he realised that the space above wasn't dark at all – plenty light came through the little round window, even half-shuttered as it was.

There was just enough headroom to sit hunched or crawl around, and there was a single shelf fitted all around the three sides that faced the window. There was almost nothing on the shelf except for a thin film of dust and, about halfway along the far wall, a stack of four thick notebooks.

Without hesitating, he reached over and took the first book.

The pages inside were filled with sketches, maps, lists of symbols and diagrams as well as paragraphs of densely-written text in his father's spiky handwriting, much of which was scored out, amended or heavily annotated. Entries were individually dated, with some running to several pages, so it clearly formed a sequential diary or journal. Pireon couldn't make sense of a single word: everything was written in some kind of code, interspersed with occasional initials.

The other three notebooks were the same, and each was filled from cover to cover. If his father had created these notebooks as he worked then there must have been a fifth book: the incomplete volume that he had been using when he died. It had presumably been lost with him.

These were what his father had felt he needed to hide.

Who was he expecting to come looking for them? Pireon wondered. And what was in them that needed to be protected? Whatever it was, his father had intended his children to find them, so he had wanted their contents to be hidden but not lost.

He carried the four notebooks down to the study and pushed the rope ladder back up through the hatch with the pole. Then he pushed the trap door shut and returned the pole to lean against the wall by the window. He removed his tabard and wrapped it round the notebooks so they wouldn't be seen: he could keep them like that, stowed at the bottom of his pack, until he left.

He might not be able to read his father's notebooks, not yet, but he would take them back with him to Elagion, where he could study them. And where they'd be safe.

2

Silvendor has returned from the east. And now he is here, at my door. With soldiers.

'My Lord.' *What else can I say?*

'Mage.'

Why is he here?

He rode fast from the Steppes. Not alone, of course. Never alone. But fast enough that the news did not precede him.

And the first thing he did, even before calling on his confused old father, was to send men to take away my staff. Soldiers, carrying a long box: the same box they made all those years ago.

Their minds were simple and they were unprepared, so when they left they believed that events had unfolded exactly the way they had planned, down to the smallest detail.

They believed that the staff was in the box they were carrying.

And now Silvendor is here. He knocked politely, of course. But he came with guards to break the door down.

What has happened?

'I have only one chair, my Lord.'

'They won't be sitting.'

The guards stay by the door, alert. And armed.

He suspects something, but what?

And how?

'I won't bore you with pleasantries.' He folds his hands in his lap, and adopts what he must imagine is a piercing stare. 'I know what you've been doing.'

What does he know?

'What I've been doing?'

'Your ships.'

My beautiful ships! He knows about my beautiful ships!

He can't know it all but I mustn't deny anything: mustn't be caught in a lie.

Can I say nothing?

'Your ships, and your soldiers …,' Silvendor pauses briefly. 'You have built a fleet that could conquer half the Inner Sea and you've done it using my face.' He sounds calm. 'You have stolen and lied. You have betrayed the trust that we placed in you.'

He knows everything. No – not everything. If he knew I'd been trying to kill the old man, I might be dead already.

But how does he know?

And how did he know that his uncle was dead?

Who is telling him these things? Who is he working with? If he is working with the black lord's enemies, are we allies?

How can I find out?

'I've seen the palace accounts, the household accounts and the Imperial Treasury reserves and I know where you took the money from. I don't know exactly how but I can only imagine that you used Hesketh, even though he remembers nothing. And that means you have a way to control him, to make him say whatever you want.'

'Yes.' *It is pointless denying it.*

I was so nearly finished – a few months only. By spring. But now, everything could be undone.

This is a disaster.

'You've been working against us …'

This is a test. The arrogant boy believes he understands everything, believes he can perhaps still use me in the future.

'Not against you, no. Never against you.' *Careful – I mustn't seem servile. I need him to pity me: to despise my weakness but not to detest me. And he must stay calm and not act rashly.*

'Then why?' he asks. 'We rescued you, cared for you, gave you somewhere safe. We do not force you to stay here, or do anything you don't want to. So why have you treated us so badly?'

What do I tell him? The truth?

'I need the ships, Lord.'

'Why? Why do you need the ships?'

'Revenge, Lord. I have enemies, Lord. You know I have enemies.'

Damn him. I was almost ready. Now everything could be ruined because someone's been talking to the idiot prince.

'You cannot use Imperial forces against your enemies, certainly not *those* enemies. But they will not go to waste. We have need of an army and a fleet in the Inner Sea, but after that we cannot afford a force of that size.'

He means to destroy them, to dismantle them, to scuttle them. My beautiful ships. Gods damn him.

'But I must decide what to do with you.'

I am too tired to flee and start again somewhere else. Not now, after all this time.

So how far will I go?

I have been pathetic since he entered the room. Now I am distraught and anguished; head lolling from side to side, eyes desperate, whining like a beaten dog.

Silvendor watches, fascinated and revolted at the same time: the young and strong and arrogant, confronted by the old and weak and broken. When the tears come, he cannot look away from that most Human thing. That unique thing.

'Forgive me.' A whimper.

He understands that it is shameful, yes. He understands that I am distraught and anguished, understands why I rise to my feet, hunched, and hobble away. I am hiding my shame from his eyes: it all seems so natural to him.

And when I reach out to the bed, that is to steady my weak and ageing frame. The bed where my staff lies waiting, concealed. Fingertips brushing the very tip is enough.

The guards at the door sway slightly as their eyes glaze

over, but they don't fall: there must be no unexpected and unexplained bruises. Silvendor is more straightforward: he slumps to one side in his chair.

Such a dangerous thing to do, and it breaks the Truce of course.

But I've done that before.

It's tricky work and risky and so much more difficult with Elves than Humans.

It is easier with touch: resting one hand on his shoulder, staff in the other. But it is still difficult.

And there is the memory.

And the memory of the memory.

And all the associations, up to our words of the last few minutes.

All gone. All clean.

How tempting to peel back his mind and discover what else he knows and how – the source. But that would be even more dangerous: risk more damage.

We still need him, Little Mouse.

At least for a little longer.

I've done too much here already, too much to hide. If anyone looks, they'll see. But who would look? Another mage, yes, but even looking would break the Truce.

Does the Damned Priest know how to look?

Who can tell what they know with their tricks and their toys: their cursed Corvak things.

When he wakes, he will say that my services will not be needed until he informs me otherwise. And I will thank him for telling me in person. And then he will leave and he will take his soldiers with him.

Hush, Little Mouse.

It's difficult enough to hide you without you making noises like that.

3

Atterlie had planned to pass herself off as a lone traveller visiting relatives, hoping to spend time among the ordinary people of Ruthin, perhaps striking close bonds and listening to their honest opinions. But from the moment anyone saw her, they assumed that she was a spy or at best an outsider.

There was something about her manner, or perhaps the way she dressed or even talked.

'You've an Arafel accent,' people said. 'What brings you to Ruthin?'

I have an Arafel accent?

She invented answers – her parents had left during the war; she had studied abroad and stayed with distant relatives; she had been working in the south and sending money home. It didn't matter what she said though, their scepticism made it clear that she had very little natural ability at such deception.

After the first three days, she chose to abandon her disguises and her stories and to simply travel as an assassin – her most practised disguise, after all – and that story was accepted without question. People looked at her nervously as they wondered who she was here for, of course, and were relieved when they heard she was only passing through.

There had been very few assassins in Ruthin since the war, they told her. Presumably personal vendettas seemed trivial and pointless in comparison with the ongoing struggle. Or perhaps the conflict provided a ready supply of armed and willing killers, without recourse to the Guild.

'I have to cross the Mountains quickly,' she explained when they asked, 'and the Gap is the only way.'

'Isn't it dangerous? With the war?'

'More than it used to be, yes. But the Gap is still the only way.'

They wished more people thought the same. More traffic through the Gate would mean more money: their whole existence would become less precarious and life might return to something like normal.

Beyond simple remarks and queries that related directly to her story, it was difficult to engage anyone in conversation. Famously, and deliberately, assassins cared for little beyond their work so even innocuous enquiries would seem suspicious. If she simply sat in one corner of a bar as a supposedly disinterested observer, no-one held much fear of talking in front of her but she had no way of prompting discussion on particular subjects. Instead, she heard a lot of talk about the vagaries of the weather, the local salacious gossip and the success or otherwise of this year's harvest.

Half a dozen times, she was jokingly asked: 'If you're an assassin, how much to kill the Duke, eh?'

She always answered without humour. 'We don't take political work.'

The geography of Ruthin also worked against her attempts to learn the mood of the kingdom. Half the population lived away from the main pass, occupying valleys that didn't lead anywhere – valleys that no-one visited without a specific reason. Isolated and inward-looking, the locals were suspicious of strangers and she found no way past that barrier.

It was a wonder that Aravan's network of agents were able to learn anything at all.

After two weeks in the kingdom, she had discovered little more than she heard on the first day: that people were less concerned with the Duke or the fighting or the soldiers on the streets than they were with the ongoing uncertainty that undermined their livelihoods.

Her time had not passed in anything like the way she had imagined.

She was particularly depressed by her inability to put anyone at their ease or to gain their trust, a skill that seemed to come to Lanvik effortlessly and instantly. Of course, she'd spent most of her life creating barriers between herself and everyone else and she had no idea if she would be able to change that. If Aravan's plan was successful, it seemed that she would cut a very remote and unapproachable Queen, standing apart from the people she ruled. Much like she remembered her father.

Her journey through Ruthin ended where she was to meet the others, at a clutch of farm buildings on a hillside above Okenbridge, in the shadow of the Cort Fells. Such a remote location was the only safe choice given the checkpoints, guardposts and occasional patrols in every town and on every road.

Two people pretending to work the fields watched her approach, before a burly farmer intercepted her on the path. 'What's your business here?' he asked.

'I heard you might need an assassin,' she replied, completing the code. She glanced down at herself, dressed entirely in black with a long blade at her side and a knife in her belt, and added: 'Clearly.'

'They'll be able to sort you out up there,' he nodded behind him. 'The building on the right, with the red door.'

'Thank you,' she said. He didn't reply.

Another four pairs of eyes tracked her route up to the cluster of buildings – one in plain view, and three behind windows. Her heart briefly sank at how amateur they were, lacking even basic training in concealment, but they had not been caught yet so she supposed their skills were sufficient for the enemy they faced.

There were a dozen people in the room behind the red door: General Aravan and three of his lieutenants, a number of the resistance fighters from Stannet and the man who had introduced himself earlier as Captain Hodier.

'I'm relieved to see you, my lady,' the General greeted her. 'Did you achieve what you wanted?' He had hated the idea of her journey and had done his best to dissuade her from it, arguing that she should stay well away from the dangers of Ruthin once her diplomatic duties were done.

'I learned as much as I was able,' she nodded.

'No problems?'

'None.'

'And our friend the mercenary?' It didn't surprise her that Aravan was still avoiding using Kiergard Slorn's name. He had spent the last few years operating across the shadowy and secretive Free Ports of the Illian Shore, so discretion would be a difficult habit to break.

'Going to plan, as far as I know.' She had travelled to the border with Slorn's Company, in their guise as musicians, though she had entered Ruthin alone, several hours after them.

'They know the timing?'

'Of course,' she told him, slightly sharply. The General had worked with Slorn's Company on several occasions: he must surely appreciate that the various resistance factions were far more likely to let them down.

Lanvik walked into the room. He had crossed into Ruthin with Aravan. 'They told me you were here!' he beamed, and they hugged.

'How are you?' She was really asking if he was still resolved to help them, to use magecraft to kill if he had to.

'Everything's fine,' he reassured her, and she pressed his arm gently.

Captain Hodier stepped forward. 'It's good to see you again, my lady.'

'And you, captain. Are you any less apprehensive about this undertaking of ours?'

'Of course not,' he admitted, after a moment's pause, 'but I will do my best to make a success of it.'

'I understand,' she said. Aravan's plan relied on resistance fighters around Ruthin standing ready to engage Imperial forces. Hodier and his people would be risking a lot by coming out of hiding: if the plan failed then they would suffer the most. But they would surely never have another chance as good as this.

'I'm certain my people would like to meet you,' he suggested. 'If you care to.'

'I'd like that very much.' She suppressed the temptation to glance at Aravan first – she didn't need his approval or his agreement.

'This way, my lady.'

Accompanied by Aravan and one of his men, uninvited, the captain led her uphill to another large and unremarkable building. Inside were around forty fighters – a mix of men and women, Elves and a few Humans. They stood spontaneously but unhurriedly when she entered, and joined in Hodier's rousing "Long live the Queen!"

Most of the voices had sounded enthusiastic; others were hesitant and sceptical.

She shook her head a little. 'Not Queen yet.'

Hodier led her among them, explaining, 'We may not have the training that your army has, my lady, but we're just as determined. We have local support, we know the ground better and we're fighting for our homes and our families.'

'I understand,' she said. 'If this goes wrong, you don't have other lives to go back to.' To these people Aravan's soldiers must seem like outsiders from far away, with no real stake in the war. Her comment attracted a number of approving nods.

As she walked among them, gauging their level of skill and training, it became obvious that most of them were identically armed. She stopped by one woman and asked, 'May I have a closer look at your blade?'

It was a well-crafted professional weapon, nicely proportioned and well balanced, with a lethal edge. It had clearly been manufactured by a large foundry rather than by some local smith, but carried no identifying marks or flourishes. There was nothing to mark it out as hailing from any particular region or kingdom, so it had been deliberately crafted to be as bland and generic as possible, by someone who worried that the arms they supplied might be traced back to them.

'These are Confederacy weapons,' she guessed, aloud. Their lack of any identifying marks had effectively served as an identifying mark.

'We take help where it is offered, my lady, especially when others have not been so generous.' Aravan had been the target of that remark. 'The Confederacy supplies us with arms and money. Sometimes training.'

'If you ally yourselves with us, will that affect your relationship with them?'

'Perhaps, but we won't be giving anything back,' he laughed.

'Do they know they've been arming so many Terevarna?'

'They've avoided asking. They may feel that it's more important that Ruthin is liberated, than who does the actual liberation.'

'Forgive the tactlessness of my question,' she apologised. 'I'm not an enthusiastic supporter of the Confederacy.'

'Not many people are, my lady, but sometimes we have very little choice who we stand with.' As well as their dealings with the Confederacy, he was referring to their current alliance. It seemed that Captain Hodier was a pragmatist and a politician as well as a soldier. He would be a useful asset in the future, if he survived.

She talked with his fighters for more than an hour, about their lives and their concerns. After a few minutes they talked more freely about why they had chosen to fight, their hopes for the future and the struggle ahead. Perhaps hearing the thoughts and feelings of ordinary people wasn't such a forlorn hope after all, if she was being open about her own identity.

It was clear that every one of them believed Aravan's main force to be far larger than it actually was. Once it arrived, they were confident that anything would be possible: any forces that stood against them could be vanquished. They had no idea that his army numbered only a thousand, a fraction of what Struving and his allies maintained in the kingdom.

Neither Aravan nor their own captain said anything to disillusion them.

They also understood that the Empire had battalions waiting in Maranth, but were confident that they would triumph as long as the Iron Gate was closed to the west.

'That's why we need to take the Gate,' one earnest fighter explained to her. 'Right up until the General's army arrives, the garrison must have no idea what's going on. That's our job: to stop any message getting through.'

'And it's not just runners – not any more,' one of his comrades added. 'That's where Edrinn went wrong. We're going to have to stop a hundred trained soldiers. At least.'

"Edrinn", not King Edrinn. She had work to do here, once the Kingdom was hers.

'Only if those men are sent. Only if the alarm is sounded.'

She didn't mention Lanvik, who would be with them. Instead she tried to reassure them, 'Hopefully you won't be needed.'

'If the Gods smile on us.'

'Perhaps the Gods are already smiling on us,' she suggested. 'Did you see the Imperial legions last week?' A few days earlier, for an entire afternoon, she had watched four Imperial legions marching from the east through the pass towards the Empire beyond.

'We talked to some of them, the conscripts,' one woman offered, 'when they pitched camp for the night. You know, for a sympathetic ear and a drink. None of them knew what was happening, and the order wasn't announced in advance. They just upped and went. Left half their equipment behind, they said.'

'The Ruthin garrisons didn't hear anything either,'

another soldier added. 'They don't know any more about it than we do.'

'Maybe there's something happening in the west, in the Empire. Maybe the Emperor died at last.'

'Whatever the reason is, we should thank the Gods for our good fortune,' General Aravan said.

Atterlie didn't say anything.

In Linnander, Kiergard Slorn had suggested that he could deal with those four legions.

'This is a big thing,' he had told her. 'If it works then you'll owe me. More than gold.'

She had agreed, of course, and promised not to mention their conversation to anyone – not even the rest of the Company – but it worried her. She knew that Slorn had Imperial connections: he had been a good friend to the Emperor's younger brother, after all. But how could he have enough influence to direct the movements of four Imperial legions? Removing them from the Steppes was effectively dismantling one of the main pillars of recent Imperial policy.

Who was it that he knew? she wondered. What was his hold over them? And why was he apparently working so hard to help her?

She was deeply uneasy about the whole situation but, as Hodier had pointed out earlier, there was sometimes very little choice about who you worked with. All around her, it was impossible to escape the tensions among the various groups, at least in part thanks to Aravan's habit of assuming a degree of authority over everyone else. She had experienced that for herself.

'Remember, we're not fighting *under* you and we're not fighting *for* you,' she had heard Hodier remind him at their first meeting, forcefully. 'My allegiance is to the house of Hengerad, some of the others not even that. But I'm willing to put our differences aside, at least until we've kicked the Imperials out.'

And everyone had drunk to that.

4

The balcony had been designed to afford superior views of deep rolling forests and the high peaks beyond, but Silvendor preferred to sit facing inwards, watching his family. From an early age, he had lived almost entirely apart from his own parents, but Oranna preferred a closer relationship with their two young children and the baby he had hardly seen. So they all shared the same suite in the palace, at least at the start and the end of the day.

At this hour Oranna, the nanny and one of the maids were occupied with cleaning, feeding and dressing the boys. In about an hour, tutors would take over responsibility for the older two.

The Crown Prince readily admitted that his pairbond's approach offered numerous advantages over his father's – he treasured the time he spent reading to the children in the evenings, for example – but there were commensurate disadvantages. This morning, he had been forced to retreat to the balcony with a mug of klava in order to prepare for the day's schedule. Even now, instead of focussing, he was slowly rotating a spoon in his mug while he watched Oranna and the children.

He had missed his family far more than he had missed the routines and responsibilities of government and the duties of Court, and their effective exile among the Hill Palaces was also high on his list of current frustrations. Not only was Arvedas no place to discharge the business of the Empire but it was no place to raise children, particularly not children who might one day assume senior roles within the greatest power in the Three Lands. Half of what they needed to learn could only be taught in the wider Court, in Emindur or Arafel: not here, among the hills and trees and the suffocating atmosphere that accompanied his Imperial Father's malaise.

He had talked with the Emperor at length the previous evening, on that subject and others. Mostly, Athendor had remained silent: when he did speak, his thoughts were muddled and unstructured. He had sounded lucid enough, more so than Silvendor had feared he might, but his attention was clearly elsewhere. Or else missing entirely.

He had met with Navin Hesketh earlier in the day, almost as soon as he reached the Imperial Compound in Mossdale. The man was limited, but that didn't mean he wasn't useful. The Emperor had once told him that every single person was like a piece on a Fugitive board, each with their own abilities and uses: the role of a leader was to combine the pieces around him, giving each a task suited to their abilities. Hesketh was more of a Castle or a Temple – a slow, defensive piece – rather than a Dragon or a Mage.

'If I may speak freely, it's good that you're here,' Hesketh told him. 'There are so many matters that require a strong hand. I can't change policy, not even as you.'

'I understand,' Silvendor reassured him, resting a hand on his shoulder. 'You've done very well, in the circumstances.'

Hesketh smiled back, gratefully.

Silvendor had read all the Council minutes and had seen "his" recommendations, but almost nothing had been authorised. The inaction was not due to any oratorical failings on Hesketh's part, but in the absence of Athendor, the Council was reluctant to commit to any course that might later prove controversial.

That was normally the safest thing to do.

Unfortunately, some matters had slipped further than they should have.

There was no rioting in the provinces, of course: no border skirmishes, no food shortages, no trade wars. The day to day business of the Empire effectively ran itself and had done for centuries. But still, there were issues that required attention.

Silvendor had braced himself for a long and difficult meeting with his Imperial Father, but their discussion had taken less time than he expected. The Crown Prince had argued that those around the Emperor must be enabled to act in his stead: given not only legal instruments to implement policy, but also the freedom to introduce new policy when required. For his part, Athendor was happy to delegate any responsibilities that he considered merely administrative but was less inclined to relinquish policy matters of any significance except directly to Silvendor.

The Emperor still required oversight, of course: regular updates, so that any decisions could be altered or simply reversed as he saw fit … judging by his lack of engagement in matters of state, that seemed an unlikely eventuality.

Silvendor was less successful on the other subject he raised. 'The business of the Empire cannot be effectively discharged from the Hill Palaces,' he had argued, 'and the Court has been here for more than a year. Since last summer.'

'And it will remain here for as long as required.'

Of course, the Court was not in Arvedas because it was *required*, because the Emperor had issued some edict. They had simply judged that their own interests would be best served by remaining close to both the Emperor and their rivals. As his Imperial Father succinctly pointed out, "What is the Court without the Emperor?"

Silvendor's work in the east would shape regional diplomacy for decades, perhaps longer, even though his lack of concrete success was frustrating, so it was imperative that he return to the Steppes as soon as was practical. Before that, now that he had the freedom to implement policy, there were a number of measures he needed to introduce.

He gathered together Hesketh and a dozen others: a mix of the Emperor's privy council and his own personal advisors: those who no doubt expected to form *his* council when he ascended the throne. These were the people he would trust with the day to day execution of his designs.

To prevent the question being raised later and to hopefully preclude further idle speculation, he started with a statement regarding the Emperor's health. 'My Imperial Father remains physically weak, though I find some reports of his condition to have been exaggerated. He is most certainly not on the brink of death and, with access to the finest medical expertise in the Three Lands, I see no reason why he will not continue on the throne for at least another twenty if not thirty years. Gods save the Emperor.'

'Gods save the Emperor,' the others chorused.

'In addition, I find my Imperial Father to be sound of mind and alert in his faculties when his attention is engaged. As he grows older, there are fewer matters in which the Emperor feels obliged to be personally involved however, and as a result, he has now elected to delegate a number of the more trivial and routine policy decisions to me. Naturally he will retain oversight at all times.'

No-one spoke. Silvendor hoped it wasn't going to be one of those meetings.

'Our alliance in the east progresses slowly,' he continued. 'Local rulers are well-disposed and vocally supportive, but there are few measurable outcomes and no commitments of any significance or substance. I intend to return to the Steppes as soon as possible.'

'Can't that work be delegated, my Lord?' Lord Brauck asked. 'Then you could spend more time here, directly engaged with the government of the Empire.' *Good – they're not just going to sit there and nod.*

'The more senior our representation in the Steppes, the greater the chance that we will achieve our goals,' he explained. 'But even when I am away, I want copies of every briefing, every decision and every order given under this new dispensation. I will stand ready to return to Court if my presence is required.'

None of them looked entirely satisfied with that

proposal, but no-one questioned it: it was a significant improvement on the current state of affairs.

'Lord Hesketh will continue in my place, as before. Do you anticipate any problems with the wizard?'

'None at all, my Lord. His mental state and overall health are fragile, but that's only to be expected considering his history. He's a bit simple – talks to himself sometimes – but he's never been anything other than loyal.'

'You trust him, then.'

'Completely. He claims to be helping us out of gratitude, but honestly – he has nowhere else to go and he believes that his enemies are still searching for him. I think he helps us because he's frightened we won't let him stay otherwise. But he'll need his staff back.'

'Of course,' Silvendor agreed. He had never felt comfortable knowing that there was a mage with a staff in the palace, but perhaps removing it had been unduly hasty. He had never planned to be here for more than two or three weeks, after all, and the mage would need his staff to resume the deception when he left. Taking it away had been something of an impulse, he assumed: in retrospect it seemed almost petty, even to him. *Passion chooses quickly, not wisely*, as the assassins said.

He couldn't be seen to reverse his decision now, of course.

'We'll return it when I leave,' he explained: 'when he needs it again.'

'He's old and sick,' Hesketh volunteered. 'He uses the staff to give him strength.'

Why has this become complicated?

'Very well. If his health appears to deteriorate, then we'll return it before then.'

Throughout the discussion, Silvendor had a nagging feeling that he had intended to talk directly with the wizard during his visit, but he couldn't recall the reason. It would surely come to him if it was important.

'My Lord ...?' Allert spoke up after a moment's silence.

'Lord Allert?'

'Perhaps we could discuss the question of our return to Emindur ...?'

Despite his own opinions, Silvendor could not be seen to have a different position to his Imperial Father. 'The Emperor believes that his health and state of mind are much improved here among the Hills, rather than in Emindur or Arafel. He will inform the Court when that changes.'

'Might it be possible for the administration to return, at least?'

'Members of the Court travel where they will, and it does not please the Emperor to force them to do otherwise. And besides,' he smiled, 'what is the Court without the Emperor?' He glanced quickly round the table, and advised, 'The matter is settled.'

They would not raise the subject again: not for some time, at least.

'Now, what's the situation with the pirate, and why haven't we dealt with him?'

'Grim Carradan,' Hesketh offered. 'We have reports of more than forty incidents in the last month.'

'More than one a day? How is that possible?'

'We believe he must be operating at least three ships, given the distribution and timing of his attacks. He mostly harries mercantile shipping, but he has also raided several towns along the Western Reach. Last month he attacked a military outpost.'

'For weapons, yes?' He had read the reports.

'He emptied the arsenal – took everything and murdered everyone he found. Several of the bodies were badly mutilated after death.'

'Almost as if he's challenging us.'

'Or mocking us.'

'Or mocking us, yes. And what is Scarthann doing?'

Scarthann, on West Durrant, was home to the Western Fleet Command.

'They've increased patrols three-fold, my lord. And doubled the garrisons along the coast.'

'Well, they need to start a sweep of the entire Durrandir Spine to flush these pirates out. And they should blockade the straits between the coast and the Spine, in sections. Stop every vessel they find.'

'The merchants won't like that.'

'They'll put up with it if they think it'll address the problem. And I want the army posting two squads and a watch at every harbour on the Western Reach, even if they have to redeploy troops from the northern frontier. Ayrgan, you co-ordinate that.'

'Yes, my lord.'

'I want details of how the Fleet will implement the change in policy and any alternative proposals they think might be more effective. Lean on them. The Western Reach is their responsibility, so let them know there's a good deal of dissatisfaction that they've let things get this bad. That should focus their attention.'

'Yes, my Lord. Do you think they'll catch him?'

'I doubt it. Not if he's smart. But I expect them to make things so hot for him that he'll sail south for easier prey. Once he's gone, I want us to be ready to move the majority of the Western Fleet to the Inner Sea: four out of every five ships, and the men with them. I want to see estimates on that – times and costs. And we'll need to berth and provision them when they arrive, ideally in our own ports rather than paying for the space.'

'The Inner Sea?'

'Last year, we could have settled the question of Arrento's hostage with gold. We didn't and as a result we look weak and indecisive. So now we have to act more forcefully to enforce the treaty.'

'How far will we go?'

'On this occasion, it might be advantageous to occupy the island for longer than after the Caldino Incident. Perhaps we could even take it into the Empire: use it as a platform to counter the Confederacy's influence in the south. At the very least we need to destroy whatever military forces they possess, as well as their merchant fleet and trade concessions. We'll sack the island and take one in four of the adult population for slaves.'

'That'll need a lot of planning. Weeks.'

'That's why I'm asking the question now. I also need briefed on the political situation: Arrento's alliances across the Inner Sea, and whether those alliances might cause us problems. I need to know anything that could affect the campaign. Who is our man in Arrento?'

'Grassett, my lord. Eorin Grassett. He's a minor noble from the south-west.'

Silvendor didn't recognise the name. 'How long has he been in post?'

'Ten years, more or less.'

'Find out why.' If Grassett hadn't requested a transfer from a dead end posting like Arrento, then he might have established local connections. It would be prudent to determine where his loyalties lay before sounding him out about their plan.

'Yes, my lord.'

'Now, … Ruthin,' he introduced the topic.

'The never-ending war,' Hesketh commented.

'I came through Ruthin on the way back and talked to a number of merchants on the road. Despite the military reports, they all agree that the situation has been growing steadily worse. Most are considering the long way round, by Eastholm or even Irlak, rather than paying to join one of the Imperial caravans. Or perhaps shipping goods by sea. So not only is the cost mounting, but our reputation suffers with every day that it drags on.'

'It's bad for morale, right across the Empire,' Brauck

nodded. 'We have thousands of troops bogged down with policing duties, apparently unable to overcome a few hundred hill farmers.'

'So what would you do?'

'We should face up to the reality that we are still at war. The local population are sheltering and supplying the insurgents, as well as providing them with fresh recruits. We need to step up reprisals.'

Hesketh shifted uncomfortably. 'Against the civilian population?'

'We need to act on a scale that will turn our enemies' own mothers against them: something to bring this to an end quickly. Executing a few dozen hostages doesn't have any effect, so perhaps we should take one thousand adults into slavery for every Imperial casualty.'

Hesketh made a sceptical, guttural noise in his throat.

'We need to be just as ruthless in Ruthin as in Arrento,' Brauck said forcefully.

'But Ruthin is *not* Arrento,' Silvendor disagreed. 'Such reprisals would damage our relations in the east, where we are already seen as the villains in the ongoing campaign. Even our allies are suspicious of both our motives and our methods. We must be more restrained, not less.'

'Much of the blame for this situation must rest with Struving,' Hesketh complained. 'The man is an idiot: too vain and self-obsessed to be effective. The task is beyond him.'

'What if we pull our own troops out, and give him enough money that he can bring in mercenaries to replace them?' Chancellor Corsham suggested. 'No doubt he would unleash them against the local population, as Lord Brauck suggests, especially if we make no move to stop him. When he's stamped out the insurgents, we can eject him and rule directly: our hands would be clean, and we could usher in a new era of peace. Many of the population might even welcome us, the second time round.'

'No-one will ever believe Struving is anything other than our man, acting on our orders,' Hesketh disagreed.

'I was informed recently that we might soon face more significant trouble in Ruthin,' Silvendor told them. 'Something much more than the usual.'

'Do you have any details?'

'Nothing. I discussed it with Struving in Ravensgill: offered to reinforce the garrison for a few months. He chose to feel insulted by the slight on his capabilities and refused the extra troops.' Silvendor shook his head. 'I thought we could move two divisions to Maranth anyway: close enough that we could be at the Gate in a few days. And perhaps a fifth legion to help secure Ruthin's eastern borders with Belsace and Rossony. For a while, at least.'

He had been sceptical of his brother's warning at the time but could think of no reason why Dalleric would lie, so he would take his own precautions to secure Ruthin.

He wished he had more specific information, but his memory of that whole conversation was oddly indistinct and slightly muddled.

5

Kiergard Slorn pulled his jacket tight about him. There was a sharp chill in the air and snow lay heaped on either side of Ravensgill's twisting cobbled streets: before long, the heavy winter snows would leave the White Mountains all but impassable. Even on the approaches to the Ruthin Gap – the solitary pass between east and west that would remain open – the weather would make any kind of movement difficult.

Captain Redwolf's timing was perfect.

Even setting aside the practical difficulties of executing military manoeuvres, the conditions would favour defence so strongly that only a madman would launch any kind of campaign in winter. Whoever held Ruthin at the end of autumn would hold it until spring: Redwolf would need those months to reinforce his position, both militarily and diplomatically.

All his senses told him that he was walking alone and unobserved, but he knew that the assassin Vy'Rhienn was following him. For anyone else, he might have made himself easier to follow – walked slower and avoided the shadows – but he was confident of her abilities. After all, with anyone else he'd have known they were there.

They had been playing at *The Five Bears* when Magda alerted him that Vy'Rhienn was in the crowd.

He hated using Magda for nothing more than collecting money from their audience, but it was the best use of her talents. Her ears and eyes were as sharp as ever, as he had told the others; the obvious point went unsaid – in her current condition, what else could she actually do?

So after they finished playing, he changed and set out alone into the night, knowing that the assassin would follow him. He hoped that she had – he had seen no sign of her.

Damn, I was trained in this and I still can't be sure she's there.

They had entered Ruthin separately – she could never have passed as a member of their troupe: nothing she did ever looked relaxed or casual, and that would have been incongruous in a company of entertainers. She would have stood out even worse than Lanvik did. So she had travelled with the Company only as far as the border.

Lanvik himself, meanwhile, was to cross later with a party of Captain Redwolf's people, several of whom were also Human. Given how strongly he felt about violence and his conviction that killing was always unnecessary, it was difficult to see how he was going to fulfil his agreement with Vy'Rhienn.

The last time they spoke, Slorn had asked him: 'You're sure you can do this?'

'I think so,' Lanvik replied, in that curious non-committal way he had. 'If it has to be done, it's better that I do it. I'll try to make sure nobody dies.'

'If anyone can do that, you can,' the assassin had assured him. She was using him, of course – using their friendship to make him do something he normally wouldn't have. All three of them understood that. And all three of them also understood that if Lanvik actually had to kill then it was not certain that he would, regardless what he had said.

'Trust no-one,' Slorn warned him. 'We won't be there to look after you.'

'And don't take any unnecessary risks,' Vy'Rhienn added. 'You don't have to be a hero.'

'I'll be keeping an eye on him,' Elisha assured them both.

Slorn doubted that was true. Although she would leave in the same group as Lanvik, Redwolf would surely have assigned her more important tasks than watching over him, given her skills and experience. But she was trying to put their minds at rest.

He had embraced Elisha when they parted and then stood watching until they were out of sight, like some forlorn pet – a puppy – but he couldn't help himself.

Why do I feel like this? Why am I completely subservient to this bond we have?

She seemed equally mystified by the strength of their attraction. The fact that they both felt the same made him love her even more.

Since then, hardly an hour had passed without him thinking of her at least once. Even now, he couldn't help wondering where she was. Most likely somewhere near Ravensgill: perhaps even with Lanvik.

The Company had crossed the border into Ruthin eighteen days ago, in their occasional guise as a musical troupe. In Darkfall they had performed in the Imperial Compound as "The Queen's Players": on this occasion they travelled as the "Minstrels of Maranth" instead, just in case.

Redwolf's agents and allies had arranged a number of bookings in provincial towns, and drummed up some interest for their first few performances. They played songs from Arvedas and Emindur almost exclusively – traditional Imperial ballads and choruses that predictably attracted some hostility even among those who were largely indifferent to the occupation. As with Imperial soldiers everywhere, however, the local garrisons welcomed any opportunity to wax sentimental. Once word had spread, it wasn't difficult to find fresh venues willing to accommodate a loyal audience with ready coin.

They were joined by Garran and Tyrell four days later. It was unclear whether their mission had been successful, but it was a good sign that neither had been detained. A few days after that, the legions from east of the Steppes had started passing through Ruthin and the Gap. Locals watched them, whispering and speculating about why so many soldiers might be on the move. According to protocol they should press on to Emindur, unless they were met by a member of the Imperial Family. At the very least, Slorn assumed, they would continue to Maranth: it didn't really matter, so long as they remained west of the Iron Gate.

After that, the Company's efforts were devoted to gradually attracting larger crowds, closer and closer to Ravensgill. For the past week, they had been performing in the capital itself – in taverns, halls and small theatres – as well as gathering information about Duke Struving and the Keep.

Their simplest plan, which had worked for them before, was to be invited to perform in the palace complex and ultimately the Keep itself. Although the physical border was only fifty or sixty miles away, this place must seem remote from Emindur: for aristocratic families as much as the common soldiery, the appeal of home and the draw of the familiar could normally be relied on.

On their fourth night in Ravensgill, it was brought to their attention that a number of senior personnel from the palace were in attendance and Slorn made a point of approaching them.

'We can also perform for smaller and more intimate audience, perhaps for his Excellency himself if he would care for the diversion?' he suggested, presenting himself as an opportunistic businessman. But no. The Duke did not feel comfortable either attending or hosting any type of social event, they learned.

Even as they pursued other approaches they also spent time scouting out the Keep, with a view to perhaps taking it by surprise or by force. Back at their lodgings, though, they quickly concluded that the Keep could not be taken unless they had the means and the will to physically tear it down. The windows were too small, the walls too exposed and too difficult to scale, and there was no access to the interior from the roof. Moreover, a number of soldiers were stationed inside at all times. With the Palace Guard based almost immediately outside and additional forces less than ten minutes away any use of force, even if successful, would endanger not just their operation but Redwolf's entire plan.

Like the Empire before them, they would need someone to open the door from inside.

Yesterday they found a coin in their takings with two "A"s scratched on it, the signal that Redwolf's forces were in place: the operation would proceed as planned, two hours after midnight, not this night or tomorrow but the night after. None of the Company had seen anyone familiar in the crowd, but they hadn't expected to.

And now, presumably because she'd heard the same news, Vy'Rhienn was in Ravensgill.

They mustn't be seen together, let alone overheard. Most of the bars and inns were surely watched at least intermittently, so he had already scouted out somewhere private to meet: a small alley on the southern slopes, behind the town's little curveball arena. It smelled bad but wasn't overlooked directly.

'Charming spot,' she commented, dropping down beside him a few seconds after he arrived.

'The smell's probably worse in summer. Were you followed?'

'No. And neither were you.'

'You slipped away from the General's people without any problem?'

'You make it sound as if I'm a captive.'

He didn't answer: Aravan, or Redwolf, needed the girl as a figurehead and would doubtless prefer her to be as far as possible from any actual fighting. 'Have you seen Lanvik?' he changed the subject.

'A couple of days ago, with the main group.'

'Well I hope he doesn't do anything risky out of friendship.' It had been bothering Slorn – it would be typical of the Human to put himself in some dramatic and dangerous situation: to pointlessly sacrifice himself.

'Honestly, he probably puts himself more at risk every

day he travels with you and your Company.'

'We rescued him from execution.'

'That doesn't change anything.'

'And Elisha?'

'I haven't seen her, but I'm sure she's close by. The Keep?'

'You're right, there's no easy way in.' They had discussed various options before setting foot in the kingdom.

'But you have a plan?'

'Struving's boys were in the audience yesterday and Lisamel's already engaged with the older lad. He'll be back tomorrow. She'll take that further, at whatever pace suits us.'

'You're certain?

'Oh, yes. He sounds like a spoiled brat, immature and naive. Easy to manipulate. That's our way in.'

'*My* way in, you mean.'

'We'll be standing ready, in case you need our help.'

'I'll be fine.'

The General believed that Slorn and his Company would be attempting to take the Keep and capture Duke Struving themselves. The princess was supposed to remain safely outside Ravensgill with one of the resistance groups, awaiting confirmation that his plan had been successful. Or not, as might be the case.

However, assuming that the Company found no way to enter the Keep without detection, she was actually paying them to get her inside. She intended dealing with Duke Struving herself.

The Company would take up positions close to the Palace. If something went wrong, they would render whatever assistance they could, but otherwise they were not to become involved.

'Your General really wouldn't like this,' Slorn said.

'No, he really wouldn't,' she agreed, 'which is precisely why we haven't told him.'

Chapter Six

The Crown of Ruthin

1

Lanvik spent the day in the town of Mannerston, where he had taken a simple room in one of the local inns.

In a few hours, he thought slowly and deliberately, *I might have to kill.*

He was immediately struck by his own choice of words: *"have to kill"*. Killing was never unavoidable so, at best, in a few hours he might *choose* to kill.

If it happened, it would be a conscious and deliberate choice to murder people whom he neither knew nor held any personal grudge against. People who were only doing their jobs, following other people's orders.

It shouldn't come to that, of course.

Their entire plan was founded on subterfuge and secrecy: if events unfolded as intended, then there would be no alarm sounded at either the Keep or any of the other targets. And if there was no alarm, then there would be no company of men dispatched to the Gate and his lethal assistance would not be required.

Standing with him against perhaps one hundred and twenty professional Imperial soldiers would be thirty or forty resistance fighters with little or no training. That was as many as could be spared: others would watch the borders, roads and junctions, checkpoints. Dozens more would deal with the hilltop beacons that ran the length of the Kingdom and which might also warn the western garrisons.

So if the soldiers came, then he would have to become involved.

Even knowing that, he still believed it was unlikely that he would have to kill them or even hurt them.

He glanced at the black instrument case that held his staff, lying on the bed beside his sword. Surely no-one would fight a mage with a staff?

The more they believe I'm a mage, the less likely they are to fight and the less likely it is that anyone will be hurt.

So he had decided to shave his head.

He had already experienced the disadvantages that would bring, of course: questions, suspicion and even hostility. But he had bought a wig and knew that, however unnatural or unconvincing it might appear, it would prevent him becoming the centre of attention wherever he went. And he would pull his hood up when he was outside, as most people did when the weather was this cold.

He towelled his head dry and examined his reflection, turning his head from left to right. Thankfully he had managed not to cut himself.

Even if the soldiers believed he was a mage, he supposed they might not feel sufficiently intimidated and if they decided to fight then he might … *choose* to kill them. No message could be allowed to reach the garrison, otherwise Aravan's men would never take the Gate; never close it against Imperial reinforcements arriving from Summerdene, Scarth and Erindale and then from further west. If that happened, then their enterprise was lost.

The local Ruthin fighters had been sceptical about his ability to affect the outcome, but Foxblade assured them that they would succeed with his help and no-one had challenged her. He had no real understanding of why they chose to put that level of trust in her – it was surely more than her title: Princess, or Queen. And his own appearance couldn't have inspired much confidence. He supposed that they wanted to believe her: wanted to have faith in what she represented.

They couldn't have known that the only uncertainty about the outcome arose from his resolve to overcome a hundred Imperial troops rather than his ability. And that resolve might be put to the test in a few short hours.

'I suppose you're happy about this,' he told his reflection, but there was no reply.

It had been weeks since his mirror-self had manifested in any way but he had kept a loose shirt on while shaving, to keep the amulet out of sight. Through the day, he kept it tucked under his clothing, safe from the people around him and safe from accidents. He couldn't risk it catching on anything.

He rinsed his razor in the sink, and laid it aside to dry.

He was to meet the others in four hours, just before midnight, a little to the west of Mannerston. He had scouted out the location already, set a little back from the highway that linked west and east, just to be certain that he knew where he was going.

He had spent the last two weeks becoming familiar with the rest of Ruthin. It was a tiny place, less than a hundred miles from side to side, and even setting aside the high peaks that were permanently covered by snow, much of it was inhospitable and barely habitable. Despite that, centuries of income from the Gate's tolls and taxes had supported a sizeable population, peaceful and prosperous until the Imperial campaign thirteen years ago and the seemingly endless violence and chaos that had followed in its wake. Passing through the Gate twice, once in each direction, had also given him an appreciation of how difficult even the simplest things would become once winter had set in.

At least a dozen times each day, he found himself wondering why he was here, doing these stupid things and taking these stupid risks. But this was where he was needed. Without him, they would need at least a hundred fighters to secure the road, whether any kind of message came or not, and neither Redwolf nor his allies could commit that number.

He was doing this for Foxblade, of course: not only

because she had asked him to, but because it would protect her. Would protect almost everyone he knew, because the entire Company was here in Ruthin and if word reached the Gate then they would be lucky to get out.

The whole business would be over very shortly and then, whatever the outcome, he would travel to Ceran'Don. He would accompany Kiergard Slorn and the others – his friends – and he would find the place they called Kylos Fern and look for Kai Arlech. Perhaps he would look for Kai Marek, who had once been his friend. And then, either alone or with allies, he would search for his enemy – the person who had stolen his memories and his life, and who had used him as an instrument of death.

It was by no means certain that he would find any of these people …

And it was by no means certain that he really wanted to, not if he had doubts about who his true self really was …

His thoughts were interrupted by a knock at the door.

He wasn't expecting anyone.

He picked up his sword. 'Yes?'

'Lanvik?' He didn't recognise the voice but he had checked in using a different name, so this was someone who knew him. He cautiously opened the door, still holding the sword.

A boy in his teens stood on the landing outside: a Human boy, half a head shorter than him, who broke into a broad smile. 'Lanvik!'

It took a moment before Lanvik recognised him. 'Geitar!'

The young lad he had met crossing the Isthmus some two years before was no longer a child. But what in the Three Lands was he doing here? He couldn't have been following Lanvik for the last two years, so he must have tracked him down somehow. More likely it was a coincidence that they were both in Ruthin: Geitar had perhaps seen him in the street.

But in that case how had he found him? Come to his door?

'Come in,' he said, leaning his sword against the wall. 'Are you on your own? Or are your parents here too?' Geitar's parents were traders, and the boy had been learning the family business.

'I'm on my own.' he shrugged expansively, still smiling.

Had he run away from home? The boy had been impressed by what he thought was Lanvik's life of adventure … could he have set off across the Three Lands alone? Lanvik didn't remember their earlier conversations very clearly, but it was quite possible that Geitar's presence was because of something he had said. He took a step forwards and they embraced tightly.

In a single move, halfway through their hug, the boy pushed up Lanvik's shirt and grabbed the amulet. He pulled it sharply down, snapping the black cord, and threw it across the room. As Lanvik heard it clatter against the far wall, he felt a sudden mist fall over his mind like a heavy curtain.

He heard his own voice saying 'Good. Now, I don't need *you* any more.'

He was no longer in control of his body, but he was still aware of his hand reaching out and drawing a long dagger from Geitar's belt.

'Get away!' he tried to shout. 'Run!'

But instead, his arm plunged the knife up and into Geitar's chest: he stepped quickly back to avoid the splash of blood. The boy's face didn't register surprise or pain or any emotion at all: it was blank and expressionless as he fell to the ground.

That was the last thing Lanvik remembered for a long time.

2

Just as she had learned knifecraft and stealth, Atterlie had been taught how to wait: rather than simply an absence of activity, waiting was an activity in itself that could be practised and improved. Without concentration, thoughts wandered and reflexes slowed: a moment's hesitation or indecision could result in an opportunity missed. Or worse.

She ran through the Guild's mental and physical exercises to help her remain alert, ready and aware as she watched from the darkness. Two hours had passed already, but the nature of their plan dictated that its timing was flexible: it would begin whenever the best moment came.

Second moonrise had been more than an hour ago, so General Aravan's forces must have struck by now: some might already have progressed to their second targets. The main army would have moved up from Mirrenlea to a ruined fortress high in the hills of Belsace where they were to camp during the day – as close as was safe to the border. And they should have set out again an hour before midnight: if everything had gone to plan then half the border posts had already fallen and communication from the others had been cut. At least some of the regular troops should be inside Ruthin.

Regardless how events unfolded through the night, they were all now committed to the General's plan.

From her vantage point outside the Keep, there had been no outward sign that anything unusual was happening at all: no bells or alarms from anywhere in Ravensgill. Not that she could hear, at least.

A number of people had entered and left the Keep through the early hours of the morning: a few civilians, but mostly uniformed Guards and messengers. There had been more than she might have expected, but she wasn't familiar enough with the palace routines to know whether this activity was unusual. Since no-one had seemed unduly alarmed, rushed or panicked, she had to assume that their numbers signified nothing untoward.

That had been earlier. Now it was after first watch and everyone inside was surely asleep. The only windows still lit by flickering torches belonged to public rooms: the private rooms and bedchambers were dark.

By the time she heard the key turn across the courtyard, light snow had begun to fall, glittering in the moonlight. She waited until she saw Lisamel at the door and then ran silently across to the awning that ran around the Keep, her footing assured on the wet flagstones. Lisamel held the thick wooden door open by a couple of inches, to let Atterlie know there was no guard standing inside. Otherwise she would have held the door open wider and lingered in conversation.

They met each other's eyes and touched hands briefly without saying anything and for a moment Atterlie felt that bond again – the closeness that the Company shared. But she had chosen a different path now and, whether this evening's adventure was successful or not, that life was now out of reach.

The night was cold and Lisamel was wearing nothing but a shift tied at the waist: the material was thin and brightly-coloured and she had presumably worn it for the evening's performance. Also, she was barefoot. She slipped quietly away into the shadows, towards the rocky embankment at the far side of the courtyard. She would meet the others past the stables, out of sight of the palace compound.

Atterlie hadn't thought to bring anything for her to wear, like a cloak to keep the damp snow off her shoulders.

When they first talked, the Company had assumed that they would storm the Keep together. When that proved impractical, they had proposed securing the door for her instead: ensuring that no-one entered or left until she was done.

But she wanted to do this alone. Needed to do this alone.

So she declined that offer, and they had suggested taking up positions around the Keep instead, on watch, but she didn't believe they were quiet enough. However hard they tried to stay still, they continually adjusted their positions. Although they believed that they would melt into the shadows around the courtyard, in practice they might be so clumsy that they alerted Duke Struving's soldiers.

She knew that she was being too critical: she couldn't expect them to be as silent as assassins. And she knew that her judgement was tainted: she was finding excuses to do this alone, without help. She was jealous of her revenge.

Passion chooses quickly, not wisely. That was what the Guild taught. Her feelings were dangerous, but if she was alert to them, then she could hopefully mitigate their influence.

So they had agreed that no more than two of the Company would watch the door from a distance, after she entered, in case she needed their help. Or, if something went badly wrong and her mission failed, then they could alert Aravan's people. If that happened, she had asked them to ensure that Struving and his family did not escape justice.

She put all thoughts of the Company aside as she stepped into the Keep and shut the heavy door behind her – not silently, but as quietly as she could. She left it closed but unlocked: she might need to leave quickly if things went wrong.

The hall inside was dimly lit and she moved quickly to a corner among the shadows. She had visualised this place a thousand times since leaving, but it felt like somewhere she had never seen before. The insignia and flags had been changed, of course, as had most of the decorative touches, but even the dimensions and the layout felt different from her memories as an eight-year old. She suppressed an uncomfortable shiver.

She heard footsteps on the stairs above, descending. Not some late sleeper moving about but, from the sound of them, three or four people.

Damn.

It seemed that there was a night watch posted within the Keep itself.

Then she heard a noise from the kitchen on the right: a door opened and three armed guards emerged. Their swords were drawn. She heard three more from the opposite side.

Ten armed men was no night watch: they were waiting for her, or someone like her.

Had Lisamel betrayed her?

No, of course not. No-one in the Company.

Someone among their allies, then: some spy in their ranks?

In that case Struving must already know about the rest of their plans.

Had Aravan's men in fact been met by waiting soldiers, and the border posts reinforced?

Was the garrison at the Gate already awake and alert?

Was their enterprise over before it had even started?

She banished those sudden distractions from her mind – she could do nothing about them, for now – and forced her attention back to the moment. There were at least ten guards, but they were slow and overconfident: if she chose to fight then she should easily reach the door unscathed and escape into the night. But she might never have another opportunity like this. And if Struving's forces weren't alerted now, then they surely would be after that.

If they already knew who she was, they would want to question her about her friends; and if they didn't know, then they would want to find out. Either way, the soldiers *shouldn't* have orders to kill her out of hand …

She stretched out her arms, with her palms forward to show that she was carrying no weapons, and stepped out of the shadows.

The guards took her sword and the long knife from her belt but didn't properly search her. Then two of them held her arms while the others sheathed their swords. Despite their uniforms, it was obvious that they had at least some Imperial training: if she broke free then they would reach for their weapons first, rather than for her, and that would give her the advantage.

They walked her up the main staircase to a pair of double doors, which two more soldiers opened: that made twelve in total. Beyond lay the audience hall, which was much as she remembered it: dark threatening columns, ancient heavy stonework and a large metal throne on a dais at the far end. Her father had always preferred the imposing atmosphere of this room to the larger and better appointed throne room in the north wing of the palace.

The new residents of the Keep apparently shared that opinion.

There were another six soldiers inside, two by the door and two on either side of her father's throne. At least eighteen armed guards inside the Keep, then, but she guessed no more than two dozen in total.

A Dark Elf sat waiting on the throne, dressed in a military tunic with a sword at his side: Duke Struving, surely. He had long thick hair, a broad forehead and appeared stockier than she might have expected for a member of the Imperial Family, albeit a distant one.

We are related, you and I.

'You, go back downstairs,' he indicated four of the guards who had escorted her up the stairs, 'in case we have any more uninvited guests.'

After they had left, the Duke smiled, apparently to himself, and stared at the floor a few feet in front of him. It was a self-indulgent drama, and she wondered who he was performing to. Was this for her? How unsure of himself he must be, if he cared about the opinions of a prisoner.

She waited for him to speak, to reveal what he knew.

'Did you really think you would catch us asleep in our beds?' he looked up, and his smile became cruel. 'You must think we're fools.'

She didn't answer, confident that he had more to say.

'We wondered who might be using the whore. An invading army, perhaps, or some band of rebels from the hills. But instead we find you, skulking at the bottom of the stairs – a girl, alone. Dressed as an assassin, but apparently working with other people – the musicians and the whore – even though Guild assassins always work alone.'

He still hadn't asked her any direct question, so she remained silent.

'And any real assassin would have chosen to kill me in some easier place than here, the best-defended building in Ruthin.' He leaned back in the throne, her father's throne. 'But if you're not from the Guild, then why are you dressed like that? Who are you, and what do you want?' He waited a few seconds. 'Well?'

From what he had said, he knew about her connection to Slorn's Company but had no idea why she was there, so he probably had no idea what was unfolding elsewhere in Ruthin.

She needed to find out how much he knew.

'I'd advise you to answer,' he prompted. 'I can assure you that you *will* tell me everything I want to know eventually, so it would be much better to talk now. If I have to use more extreme methods, then by the time you regret your silence it'll be too late.'

'How did you know I was coming?' she asked. The question invited him to boast about how superior he was and how clever he'd been.

'Excellent,' he leaned back in the throne a little: 'we're going to have a conversation after all.' He smiled without any real humour: 'It's ironic that you thought you'd use my own son against me. Vinderich may be a fool, but he is a dutiful fool: he keeps me well-informed of anything suspicious or unusual, particularly anything that involves women or gambling. His own judgement in those fields has proven to be unsound in the past, you see. So I heard all about his new *friend* and the musicians she works with …'

It seemed that they hadn't been betrayed. It was simply that Kiergard Slorn's plan had been too transparent, and the boy not as stupid as he seemed.

'… and on the very night their whore charms her way inside the Keep, the musicians slip out of their accommodation and take great care not to be followed. To be honest, we were expecting her to let *them* in but instead we get you, whoever you are. I don't know what you're doing or who you're working with, but I've alerted the garrison at the Iron Gate. Whatever you've planned, you and your friends, will not be allowed to happen.'

Even if Struving didn't know anything, had been guessing, it was a disaster if a message had been sent to the Gate. She had seen soldiers enter and leave the Keep earlier, and had no reason to believe that he was lying. Why would he? She was already his prisoner.

Had her adventure in the Keep, her drive for personal revenge, compromised Aravan's plan and exposed his forces? Ruined everything?

If troops had been despatched to the Gate – a half company, according to what she knew – then everything now depended on Lanvik. Had he been in place, ready? And had he been able to overcome his qualms and act?

She put the question aside: she had no way to affect that now, and she needed to address the situation right here. Struving's confidence would make him sloppy but she had to stay alert if she was to take advantage of that.

'So,' he continued, 'will you tell me where your friends have gone? Or will you lie, and tell me that you don't know?'

'They're just mercenaries,' she shrugged. 'I paid them to get me into the Keep. They probably expect me to be captured, so they've left Ruthin as quickly as possible.'

'*You* paid them? So this is about you? You're working alone and your goal was to get in here?' He shook his head.

'Not very convincing, I'm afraid. Why would any one person go to such lengths and risk so much just to stand where you're standing now?'

'My name is Vy'Rhienn,' she told him. 'Your men murdered my father in this place, and tonight I've come to take back my kingdom.'

A number of the guards froze momentarily or glanced across to her. There was an almost imperceptible delay as Struving took in her words. Then he laughed: 'At last, the missing princess comes home! Unfortunately, I think you'll find that Ruthin is no longer *your kingdom*.'

'Ruthin is mine, as it was my father's before me and his father's before him,' she disagreed. 'And it is certainly not *yours*: you are a puppet, with no real power – what are you, a *Duke*? That throne was given to you as a reward for murdering my family.'

'Not all your family,' he retorted. 'Not you, clearly, and not your mother … though I heard recently that the Princess Arenima had been murdered. In her own home. That was you, I assume?'

'She came to Ruthin using trickery and deceit. She pair-bonded with my father under false pretences. And when the time was right, she arranged for his death and the deaths of her own children.'

'Is that what you thought?' Struving smiled. 'Your mother certainly didn't arrange all of that: didn't even know what we were going to do, you stupid child. She believed we would lock you all up – take you hostages to ensure your father's good behaviour – or perhaps deport you to live the life of minor nobles somewhere in the provinces. She'd never have helped us otherwise. She loved your father: why would she have helped us kill him?'

Damn.

When they had talked last winter, everything her mother said had reinforced the idea that it was *her* strategy to gain influence over Edrinn, and later to depose and execute him and their five children. All with the aim of ending Ruthin's traditional neutrality and handing the kingdom to the Empire.

Why didn't she tell me?

Even at the end, she wouldn't speak against her damned family and its Empire.

'It seems to me that there are a number of problems with your story,' Struving returned to his questioning. 'Even if you are the old king's daughter, why would you work alone? Slipping into the Keep and murdering everyone here would not deliver Ruthin to you, so there must be more to your plan than that.'

She didn't answer. For all his exaggerated delivery, he was no idiot.

'And in that case, I assume you have more allies than your handful of mercenary musicians. Have you perhaps convinced some of the rebels that you are their Queen?'

When she still didn't speak, he continued, 'You're my prisoner, but everything about you – your voice, your face, your insolent manner – indicates that you do not believe yourself defeated. And that tells me that your presence here is only one part of your plan.' He leaned forward: 'But it doesn't matter how many friends you have, little princess: the Empire will never surrender its access to the Steppes.'

'The Empire has already withdrawn from the Steppes,' she assured him. 'Didn't you see the legions?'

'They'll be back.' Struving didn't look even mildly discomfited: he exuded a supreme and arrogant confidence.

'On the contrary, I have been promised that they will not be returning. Certainly not soon.' That was a lie, of course: she had no idea how Slorn had influenced the legions or how long it would be before they discovered his deception and redeployed.

Struving looked a little unsure of himself for a moment.

If she had allies who could control the movements of four Imperial legions, then he might be dealing with more than one deluded girl and a rabble of local fighters. There might be political implications for him to consider. His own position may have been created by the Imperial Family and the Court, but would they have moved those four legions if *he'd* asked?

His hesitation was fleeting. 'Those particular forces might be needed elsewhere, but there are thousands of trained troops stationed here in Ruthin. I'm afraid that anyone you've persuaded to fight against us will only be making themselves an easier target than when they hide in the shadows. We've been looking for an opportunity to defeat these people in a proper campaign for years, and you may have given us just that.'

Struving's whole performance was becoming gradually more self-indulgent and more melodramatic. Soon he would reach the point when he either ordered her taken away or had her killed on the spot: that would be the moment that she had to act. She didn't reply but let him continue.

'It's hard to believe that you've worked towards this for thirteen years,' he laughed, 'and this is the way it ends. It's pathetic. I'm almost tempted to keep you alive long enough to witness the collapse of all your plans, just so you understand that you never stood any real chance of success. But every moment you're alive gives some hope to my enemies, however slender, that your particular vision of Ruthin might prevail.'

Almost …

He leaned back in the throne. 'Our little chat has been absolutely delightful, my dear. I've enjoyed it more than you would believe. But I have other things to do now, starting with hunting down your allies.' He nodded to his men: 'Kill the girl.'

The soldier on her left was the leaner and faster of the two: his hand started tightening on her arm before Struving had finished talking, so she killed him first. She had a blade in each sleeve, released with a wrist trigger, and she half-spun to her left as she released them. The blade in her right hand sliced across the guard's throat, at the same moment as the blade in her left hand cut the hamstring of his slower companion.

She had straightened back up, adopting exactly her previous position and posture, by the time Struving finished saying "girl". The effect might only annoy the Duke, but it would make his men a lot more hesitant about attacking her than they had been a moment before.

A moment later there was a crash, as the guard to her left crumpled dead to the floor; the guard to her right sank to one knee and started screaming. She reached across and quickly slit his throat: he stared at the blood spurting from his neck and reached up to it with both hands as if to stem the flow, before collapsing to one side. His head and chest spasmed slightly before becoming still.

There was complete silence in the hall for a moment, before Struving screamed: 'Kill her!' He pointed to where Atterlie had been standing, but she wasn't there any more. She was running diagonally across the hall, and throwing the three light blades from her jacket. Still not adjusted to the changing situation in the hall, the guards stood conveniently immobile, attempting to dodge only at the last moment. One of the blades was completely effective; the other two at least caused injuries.

By the time Struving shouted, she had removed a length of threadwire from her hair and was only five or six feet from a sixth guard. She slid into his shins while he was drawing his sword and as he fell she reached up, slipped the wire over his head and used his own momentum to slice halfway through his neck.

She grabbed the handle of his sword, already halfway out the scabbard, intending to arm herself, but it was too badly balanced for her to use effectively so she tossed it aside. She should have retrieved her own sword instead.

The guards were moving now, lumbering towards her

for the most part, slowly enough that she had time to unclip the short blades from her wrists and throw them at the nearest. They weren't designed as throwing weapons but were well enough weighted that both found their target – one in the upper chest and the other in his face: sufficient to remove him from the fight, at least for now.

That left five fully able soldiers – two by the door, one to her right and two to her left.

They were slow, but they had numbers of their side. She mustn't be overconfident; mustn't be sloppy and make stupid mistakes; mustn't let them establish a position in which they could overwhelm her. Right now, she was improvising: despite all her training, she had never been properly taught how to fight a group of enemies. No assassin should ever need those particular skills.

She hadn't stopped running, and now she wheeled towards the isolated soldier on her right, drawing two stiletto blades from her boots. Shifting her weight and her balance from foot to foot, she ran straight towards him, holding the blades low. She couldn't miss the fear in his face – he had seen seven of his comrades killed or wounded in as many seconds, and now she was coming for him. He didn't know whether to run or fight and his indecision made him another easy target: his sword might have been raised, ready to parry her attack, but his eyes were darting around looking for somewhere to run. She feinted to his right and when he moved his arm to block, she came inside it with her other knife and caught him in the chest. As he reeled, she shouldered him and followed through into his stomach with the knife in her left hand. He fell backwards to the floor and his sword clattered away from him.

She couldn't leave the injured soldiers alive, couldn't afford the possible distraction later, so without breaking stride she turned towards them. They were hurt and slow and she was moving at speed, so they had no chance. They should have joined the others: isolated like that, they were vulnerable and easy to pick off one by one.

She had no more ways to surprise the remaining four soldiers: they knew she was armed, they knew she was fast and they knew she was going to attack. But she had traded all of those for the advantage of fear – they had just seen their comrades dispatched, easily. If they were as scared as the young lad on the other side of the hall, then they would be hesitant and defensive: slow.

She had to deal with them quickly, before they thought to summon help from their comrades outside or to raise a more widespread alarm.

They had moved closer to each other, but hadn't realised that they had the advantage. There were four of them and they were all armed, whereas she had used most of her weapons: all she had were the two stiletto knives in her hands. They should have rushed her as a group, but instead they kept their distance.

How badly had these soldiers been trained?

She assumed they were Struving's own people, rather than Imperial guards. Were they so wary of her that she had time to retrieve her throwing blades …?

Her thoughts were interrupted when Duke Struving lunged at her.

She had heard and seen him rise from the throne of course but only at the periphery of her awareness, and she'd disregarded him as a threat. His attack came as a complete surprise, even though she had known he was near. He thrust at her with his sword and she danced backwards, well aware that she couldn't afford a prolonged duel with others in the room.

His third move was a feint, so easy to read that it was almost a parody of the move it pretended to be. She turned inside his sword arm and planted both of her knives in his chest. It had been easy, but from the start she had wanted to take him alive.

She could have knocked him unconscious and spared

his life, but instead she had chosen to kill him. She could have blamed the heat of the moment or the fact that he had surprised her, but those were only excuses. It would have taken very little effort *not* to kill him.

Damn.

She gathered up his sword, which was a far better weapon than his soldiers were equipped with.

With Duke Struving dead, of course, the four remaining guards had even less reason to fight.

She held the sword lowered and unthreatening and walked slowly around the hall, pausing at some of the bodies to retrieve her throwing blades, as she addressed the four guards: 'You can still walk away from this alive. I have no reason to want you dead. I came for Struving, not for you: you're not my enemies. If you're prepared to lay down your swords now, then I have friends coming and they'll look after you and …'

They wanted to believe her so they let her come closer, even though they had just watched her collect her three knives. But this was no time to be merciful: as soon as she was close enough to be reasonably certain of the kills, she attacked. She caught the first two each with a blade in the middle of their foreheads, but the third had started moving before she was able to throw. The knife embedded itself in the side of his head instead – even if the wound hadn't been immediately fatal, he would not survive it for long and would take no part in the struggle.

The last soldier had time to adopt a defensive position, but she could see from his eyes that he had no belief in his ability to stop her. She feinted once with Struving's sword and when he parried, her knife slipped easily past his guard.

She glanced around. The hall was secure, but she had to make sure that no-one raised the alarm. There were more guards in the Keep: at the very least, two outside the door and the four that Struving had sent back downstairs, but quite possibly others. Moreover, there had been no sign of

Struving's family so far, and there would be household staff in the building as well.

She was alive and Struving was dead but there were still too many unknowns for her to be safe.

In retrospect, this was the point when she would have appreciated the Company's assistance. She had assumed that her enemies would be asleep, though, and had told Slorn to wait and not to interfere. The main door was still unlocked, though, so they could easily enter the Keep. But they didn't know that.

She lifted one of the torches from its bracket on the wall, walked over to the narrow west-facing window and waved it from side to side: one long and two short. She repeated that pattern three times. She hadn't agreed any signal with the Company but she knew that they used that sequence themselves. If they saw it, hopefully they would understand what it meant. And hopefully it wouldn't attract the attention of any of Struving's men.

She couldn't delay, of course: couldn't assume anyone was coming. She took a few seconds to wipe her blades and tuck them away again and then she retrieved her own sword, which was far lighter than Struving's. Finally, she opened the thick double doors that led to the small landing: two guards were waiting there, one on either side, just as they had been when she'd been brought up.

'You're to go inside,' she told them calmly.

'What?' one of them asked, puzzled.

Although they didn't understand what was happening, her relaxed manner made them drop their guard. Not realising that they were at risk, their reaction to her was one of confusion instead of caution or alarm, and they let her come far too close.

Almost the first lesson they taught at the Guildhouse was that an assassin's best weapon was surprise. Most of her training had been founded on the assumption that her target would be unaware that they were about to be attacked, so by establishing that element of surprise she had made her two kills easy.

Easy, but not perfect.

She was needlessly clumsy and one of the soldiers fell away from her: his sword clanged on the flagstones and his body fell with an audible *thump*.

A moment later there was a call from downstairs, 'What's happening up there?'

She briefly considered dragging the two bodies inside the hall to conceal them, but there was too much blood on the floor for an effective ambush. She would have to deal with the four soldiers directly. She wished she'd brought a bow, to take advantage of her higher ground: she would have to make do with her throwing blades.

'What was that noise?' the voice insisted. One of the soldiers was climbing towards her, alone.

She couldn't fight him on the stairs with a blade: even if she was more skilful, his upwards reach would be more effective. Instead she waited in the shadows for him to come closer. His gaze was fixed on the open door to the audience hall straight ahead and he only noticed the bodies on the floor when he was two steps from the landing. Only a few feet from her. She took advantage of his brief surprise and then caught and lowered his body quietly to the ground, before pulling it away from the top of the stairs.

'Tarran?' one of the soldiers downstairs called up. He moved to the foot of the stairs and put one foot on the bottom step: 'Tarran?'

Splitting up when they were facing an unknown enemy was a stupid mistake, but they were apparently determined to come up the stairs one at a time and let her pick them off. Unfortunately, simply waiting for them would be too risky: at any moment they might decide to call for help or to alert the garrison. So she had to go to them.

She took a measured breath to centre herself, and then skipped as casually as she could down the stairs. They stared at her, confused but wary, with their weapons drawn. They might not have been fooled but they were hesitant and unsure, which gave her a chance to study them – how they were armed and exactly where they were standing.

Eight steps from the bottom, she vaulted over the banister and rolled to a crouch on the floor, drawing her throwing knives. The nearest soldier was easy to pick off, but the second was alert and expecting her blades, so they struck lower and less precisely. He was wounded badly enough that he only offered a couple of weak parries when she closed and dispatched him with her sword.

By that time, the third soldier was upon her and she found herself in precisely the kind of sword fight that she'd hoped to avoid. After a few seconds, though, they heard a loud anguished scream from upstairs, from the audience hall. Unable to stop himself from reacting, her opponent's eyes flicked briefly towards the stairs.

The distraction was enough for her to catch him inside his guard and run him through.

Dimir's breath, it was as if they hadn't trained at all.

She wiped her sword quickly on his jacket, turned and ran back up the stairs to investigate.

The scream had been loud enough that it would surely have woken anyone in the Keep who was sleeping, so it would certainly have alerted any remaining guards. The voice had been female – Dark Elf – and Atterlie guessed it belonged to Struving's pairbond, presumably having discovered his body. She had no idea who else might be with her – the rest of the family, or perhaps more soldiers – so she climbed the last few steps more cautiously.

There was no-one on the stairs or the landing and the doors to the audience hall were still wide open. She walked quietly through them with her sword raised. The five people inside, two of whom were armed guards, came together as a group when they saw her. The other three would be Struving's family: his pairbond the Duchess and his two sons. The older youth, Vinderich, was a little younger than her but would still remember the time before they came here. He stared at her, angry and wild. The other boy, Girbek, was too young to have known anything other than Ruthin. He looked dazed, as if he didn't understand what was happening.

Both boys were armed and the older boy looked ready to rush forwards and attack her.

Whatever I do with them must be born of reflection, not anger or hatred, she told herself.

'What have you done with our father?' Vinderich demanded. The signature rasping deep in his chest showed the strength of his emotions: in this state, he might well do something unwise.

This was not the time for a flippant comment, so she answered with the plain truth.

'He attacked me and I killed him. The Struvings no longer rule here.'

The boy tried to push towards her but his mother and the two guards stopped him. For all his fury, he didn't press against them.

She assumed that these guards were as ill-prepared and ill-trained as the others had been, so any contest should still favour her, even without the advantage of surprise. But there was no point taking unnecessary risks.

'I have no quarrel with you,' she addressed them directly. 'Your comrades are dead but there is no need for you to join them. There would be no dishonour if you stood down: I am a Guild assassin – you are not my equal.'

After a moment's indecision, the guards lowered their swords: they were still drawn, ready to defend their three charges, but the message was clear.

Atterlie knew that she should kill Struving's family. Alive, they gave the Empire an excuse to intervene again and they would be an obvious focus for resistance among any who favoured Imperial rule in Ruthin. They might even vanish into the Empire and spend long years preparing their revenge, just as she had done.

If their positions were reversed, they would have killed her: *had* tried to kill her, of course, all those years ago. But their situations were not the same: these three were not alone and friendless. Across the Empire, there were families who would care for them: give them another life.

Also, if she killed them, she would have to kill the two guards, and she had no appetite for that.

'This was my home,' she addressed the boys, trying to explain, 'until soldiers came in the night to kill my father. I should kill you right now, but I had an older brother and sister who were your ages, more or less …'

But it was pointless talking to them. They stared back at her stonily, angry, not listening or understanding what she was saying.

'Enough people have died here,' she started again. 'You will be detained until the situation is more settled and then I will have you escorted to Imperial territory. If I ever see you again or hear that you have made any claim to the Crown of Ruthin then I will either kill you myself or I will send someone to kill you.' She turned to the guards: 'Take them back to their rooms and make sure they stay there. If you do that, you will be given safe passage away from here. But if you or they emerge before being sent for then you *will* die and so will they.'

The two guards nodded curtly, efficiently, and led Struving's family away by the back stair that led to the royal suite above. The woman was stoical and silent, almost in tears, but Vinderich left shouting angry obscenities back at her. The younger boy followed in silence.

So, she reflected, she had decided to let them live.

She had always assumed that she would be consumed by the urge to avenge her family – would have to struggle not to let her cold anger triumph. But she knew that she had succumbed to emotion after all, by letting them live. They would always be a threat to her, however slight, so she should have killed them now when she had the opportunity. But some part of her had needed to prove, *I am not like you.*

When the hall was silent again, she turned towards the landing.

'Come out here where I can see you.'

She had seen a flicker of movement out the corner of her eye, had heard cloth brush against stone: someone was standing behind one of the doors, trying not to be seen.

'Come out,' she repeated. 'I saw you a moment ago. I know you're there.'

A Terevarna woman stepped into view: perhaps thirty, dressed in servant's clothes.

'Fetch the household staff,' she ordered. 'Everyone in the Keep who isn't family. Quickly.'

The woman returned with another five servants a few minutes later: two Light Elves, two Dark Elves and a Human. Most looked as if they'd only just woken up. They stood in the doorway, staring in shock at the bodies strewn across the floor, including the Duke. Struving had presumably not informed them of his plans for this evening, just as he had presumably not informed his own family.

They would be hand-picked and loyal, so she could not let them leave. Not yet.

'I have no reason to harm any of you, but you have to stay here in the Keep for now,' she told them. 'There is more fighting taking place across Ruthin, but someone will let you know when it's safe. I need to you go back to your quarters now and wait until someone comes for you.' She looked along the line: most of them looked away but a couple held her gaze. 'Go.'

They withdrew without saying anything.

She hadn't given them any indication how long they might have to wait, but even if the General's plan was on track it would be another three or four hours before his men might have time to check on the Keep.

She had no idea what was happening outside, across Ruthin – whether the bulk of Aravan's army was now securing the kingdom, and whether Lanvik had overcome his moral scruples and stopped the Duke's messengers. Here in the Keep, though, everything had gone as well as she could have hoped. Struving and his guards were dead; his family and the staff cowering in their rooms.

To be thorough, she should search the rest of the building in case anyone else was hiding, but it was pointless putting herself in any new danger. No-one would emerge to threaten her, not if they hadn't already. And she wanted to avoid adding to the night's tally of deaths. There had been enough killing: more than when her family were murdered, she was sure.

It had not been the most pleasant start to her reign.

She walked across the hall, avoiding the sticky pools of blood, and sat on the throne at the far end.

Queen Vy'Rhienn.

She couldn't resist a bittersweet smile.

The last time I sat on this throne, my legs didn't reach the ground.

She heard a loud imperious knock from downstairs: wood on wood. The outside door.

As soon as she heard the sound, her first thought was that she had left the main door to the Keep unlocked.

Damn! Damn! Damn!

It had seemed the right thing to do when she entered, providing her with a quick way out and allowing easy access for Slorn's people and the General's forces. But the Company had not followed her in and the General's army was still hours away.

The only people that the unlocked door would give easy access to were her enemies.

She had been stupid: she should have locked herself in from the start.

At the very least, she should have locked the door once

she'd overcome Struving's guards. But she'd been thinking like an assassin and leaving an escape route after her kill, rather than thinking like a soldier and securing her position.

She had left herself vulnerable.

She rushed down the stairs but it was already too late: the heavy door swung open before she was halfway down and a group of uniformed men walked in. They were armed and ready, prepared for violence: from the lack of any answer and the fact that the door was unlocked, they already knew something was amiss.

'You! Come here!' the single officer beckoned. From his insignia, he was a Captain in the Imperial Guard and his eleven men were dressed in Imperial uniforms rather than Struving's colours. Despite the uncertainty, they were relaxed and disciplined: secure in their own abilities. This would be a much more dangerous situation than earlier if she chose to fight, so hopefully she wouldn't need to.

She sheathed her sword.

She had no idea why they were here: perhaps to relieve the night watch? Perhaps a random patrol? If they had learned of a threat to the Keep or if an alarm had been raised, then they could have sent a hundred men. The fact that there were only twelve surely indicated that Aravan and his men were still undiscovered.

So far …

'Who are you?' the Captain asked, apparently unflustered by the three corpses on the floor.

'Princess Vy'Rhienn,' she told him. He didn't react to the name: perhaps didn't recognise it, in which case he might assume that she was simply a house guest. Except that she was dressed as an assassin: all black, and spattered in blood.

'Where is the Duke?'

'Upstairs.' He didn't react to that either.

'I've sent word to the barracks,' he informed her. 'More troops will be on their way. Whatever's been going on here, we'll get it sorted out.' He sounded practical and confident.

'I'm afraid not,' a familiar voice disagreed. Kiergard Slorn walked through the still open door with his sword raised, accompanied by most of the Company. 'The man you sent will not be able to deliver his message.'

'Whoever you are, you've made a mistake,' the Captain responded. 'Stand down, now!' He and his men raised their swords.

'Wait!' Atterlie interrupted loudly. 'This would be a stupid fight: nine against twelve, with no clear outcome. There's no point.'

Slorn said nothing, but something in his expression indicated that he believed the outcome would have been perfectly clear.

'No point?' the Captain prompted.

'Beyond these walls, a struggle for Ruthin is taking place,' she explained. 'Our forces should already control the borders and the Gate. We have hundreds of troops in place and our soldiers will join us at the Keep in a couple of hours. If we have failed, then your soldiers will reach the Keep instead, in substantial numbers. In either case, one of our two groups will be hopelessly overwhelmed.'

'You're suggesting we simply wait?'

'It would avoid unnecessary bloodshed.'

'How do I know what you're saying is true?' the Captain asked.

'It doesn't matter. If I'm inventing this, then more of your people will be here to relieve the Keep in a few hours anyway,' she told him. 'You have nothing to lose.'

'Very well,' the Captain agreed with a slow nod. 'We wait. But we leave the door unlocked.'

'Agreed.'

'And the Duke?'

'The Duke is no longer relevant.' The Captain nodded. He knew exactly what she meant. 'And these three?' He indicated the bodies on the floor.

'You can move them if you want. I didn't have time.'

'We'll wait over there,' Slorn said, indicating the left hand side of the hall. He sheathed his sword and most of the Company followed his example. The Imperial guards took up station by the opposite wall. Both groups tried to make themselves as comfortable as possible while remaining alert.

'Lanvik would be proud of you,' Vrosko Din commented. 'You stopped us hacking each other to pieces.'

'He wouldn't be if he knew how many people I've killed tonight.' No, Lanvik would have been ashamed of her. She had made more kills in the last twenty minutes than in her entire career as an assassin, but it wasn't simply the numbers: it was the way she had treated her enemies. She had been ruthless. Merciless.

And, of course, she hadn't arranged this truce in order to save any lives either. Aravan's plan relied entirely on secrecy, rather than force of numbers, and this was the only way she could be completely certain that no alarm would reach the barracks. Even if Kiergard Slorn's Company prevailed, a lone soldier escaping into the night could turn the outcome of their entire enterprise. She couldn't take that risk.

'Are there other soldiers in the Keep?' Garran asked, quietly.

'There are two guards upstairs with Struving's family, but they should stay out of our way. Have you heard anything from the others?'

'We've been out there all night. We haven't seen anyone else. You?'

'Struving saw through your ruse: he sent men to the Gate earlier.'

'That's not good.'

'I know. I'm worried about Lanvik.'

'He'll be fine,' Vander reassured her, but none of them knew how events had actually played out on the road: how Lanvik had fared against half a company of Imperial soldiers. She had hoped that he wouldn't be needed, but now they were all relying on him.

As the hours passed and there was no noise from outside other than the occasional sound of birds, they became bored and distracted. Kiergard Slorn in particular was apparently unable to settle: he paced back and fore like a caged animal.

'I don't like being shut in here,' he said, when she tried to persuade him to sit down. 'I understand why you've arranged things like this, but it puts the fate of the entire Company in the hands of other people. And in my experience, other people usually let you down at the worst times.'

'I feel exactly the same,' she agreed, quietly, 'but we have no choice.'

From the earliest days of her training, she had been taught to be dependent on no-one: not to leave herself vulnerable to the actions or inaction of others. Like Slorn, she was confident she could have fought her way to safety: simply sitting here and waiting felt uncomfortably like surrender. She tried to reassure herself: there had been no alarm and the forces in the Keep had been ignorant of any attack, so the General's plan must be unfolding in their favour.

Mustn't it?

She wasn't completely reassured by her own logic.

It was almost dawn before they eventually heard the sound of dozens of boots crossing the courtyard outside. There was a loud knock on the door.

The Captain and Slorn looked at each other sharply and their hands drifted back down to their weapons.

Atterlie stood, forcing herself to at least appear calm. 'I'll answer it.'

As she covered the handful of steps to the door, she rehearsed in her mind what she would do if she found Struving's men outside. Her left hand was waiting to trigger the blade in her sleeve and once she had started pulling the door open, her right hand would drop towards the knife at her hip. She would have surprise on her side: if she was lucky, she could cut a route through them. Her best chance of escape was probably through the south wing.

As she opened the door, though, she found herself face to face with General Aravan. His own sword was in his hand, ready. Forty or fifty soldiers stood with him, all in the colours of Ruthin. It seemed that his army had successfully crossed the border and at the very least was operating freely in Ravensgill.

She smiled warmly, but he was angry. 'We agreed that you would not risk yourself,' he told her: 'that you would stay away from the Keep.'

She stepped aside to let him in, and he continued: 'As soon as I learned of your disappearance, I expected to find you here. You or your corpse. What a stupidly dangerous thing to do. Is any of that blood yours?' Her clothes were spattered with dried blood.

'No.' She indicated the Imperial soldiers, standing in a group with their hands resting on the handles of their swords. 'These gentlemen have been very reasonable. I have guaranteed them safe passage to the frontier.'

'Very well,' he agreed: 'When things have settled down.' He turned to Kiergard Slorn. 'Why did you let her do this?'

'She seemed very confident,' Slorn shrugged. 'And she's paying us.'

'Struving?'

'Dead,' she told him. 'By my hand.'

'And who else is in the Keep?'

'Struving's family and two guards. Upstairs. They also have safe passage. The household staff should also be waiting in their rooms. I've seen no sign of anyone else, but that's no guarantee.'

'Secure the building,' he instructed the men filing into the Keep, dressed in Ruthin uniforms. 'Check every room, and bring the Duke's family and their guards down here. Be careful. And someone get our flag up.' There was a flagpole at the top of the Keep, which would still be flying Struving's family arms.

Aravan must have brought a flag with him, then.

For all that he had objected to her focus on Struving and the Keep, he appreciated how important the symbols of power were. The flag would be a signal to everyone who saw it, far more effective than any handbill or proclamation. And he would have brought clothes for her, no doubt, rich in the regalia of Ruthin.

After thirteen years, she could finally put the assassin to one side: Atterlie's work was done. But she had one more question before that, an important question: 'Struving sent men to the Gate. Have you heard anything from Lanvik?'

'Not from him or the men he was with, my lady. It's unfortunate that they were needed, but I'm sure he will have done what he promised. When our men reach the Iron Gate, they will take the garrison completely by surprise. Don't worry: the Crown of Ruthin is secure.'

'The Crown of Ruthin has changed hands twice in the last fifteen years, and everyone in the Three Lands will soon be aware of that fact,' she disagreed, with a shake of her head. 'I fear it is anything but secure.'

A Short Glossary

Selected Names and Places Mentioned in the Text

Abyrne – town on the Great River, in Morven in the Northern Steppes

Adastana – Pireon's older sister, known as "Dasha"

Aistolea – one of the Floating Cities of Corvak, lying west of Elagion

Ajiila – trainee Dancer on Elagion, close friend of Pireon and former focus of his romantic attentions. Now betrothed to his brother Dach

Alaion – city in Corvak's Delta

Aldarian Guard – former elite unit in Ruthin, headed by General Aravan

Alekteria – Pireon's paternal grandmother

Amphet – younger cousin of Quiron, who lives on the Kayoden estate with his pairbond Ilada and their three children

An'Holt - military installation in the Confederacy, from which Kiergard Slorn stole the Ruby Hand

Father Anthedon – Priest and agent of the Hierarch, appointed to the Embassy Temple in Emindur. Accompanied the Imperial Court to the Hill Palaces

Dark Aoshay, the Formless – one of the Twelve Gods of Corvak, the God of Shapes, Puzzles, Treachery and Luck

Arafel – the Winter Capital of the Empire, presumed to be the largest city in the Three Lands with over one million souls

General Aravan – former head of the Aldarian Guard in Ruthin, more recently operating as a pirate captain known as Redwolf

Ardendar – the middle sized of the three moons. The Red Moon

Queen Arenima – pairbond of King Edrinn. Allowed Imperial soldiers into the Keep, during the fall of Ruthin. Killed by her daughter Vy'Rhienn's at Penarch House

Armandir – an Illian God believed to live in water

Arrento – an island in the Inner Sea. Vander and Aruel hail from Arrento

Aruel – Vander's lover, a lady of the Fassiori of Arrento. Killed by Kiergard Slorn in An'Holt

Arvedan Hills – south-west of Emindur, home of the Hill Palaces to which the Imperial Court sometimes relocate

Asfahal – one of the Twelve Gods of Corvak: the Goddess of Love and Desire, the Lady of the Two Loves

Emperor Athendor the Eighth – the current Emperor

Atterlie – name used by Princess Vy'Rhienn as an Assassin. Her Chapter Name is Foxblade

Avellador – coastal state bordering the Confederacy

Bane – giant Madarinn member of Kiergard Slorn's Company

High Belluhar – one of the Twelve Gods of Corvak

Black Rat – one of the Nine Clans, the clan of Sailors and Travellers

Brothers of Duraxi – worshippers of Durac and the Book of Duraxi, which exists in several different versions

Calinnia – small island in the Inner Sea, home to a fishing village of the same name and Davata Lodge
Grim Carradan – a pirate operating along the Empire's Western Reach
Carissola – largest island in the Inner Sea, and roughly central within it
Ceran'Don – the mountainous Eastern Continent, also known as the Land of Mists. The homeland of Humans and mages
Cerinium – Large city in Darrenby, where the Eastern and Western Branches of the Great River merge
The Circle of the Twelve – ancient round stone building at the centre of the Elagion, containing statues of the twelve Gods of Corvak
Clans – Terevarna society is divided into nine Clans: each Clan has its own leaders, rituals, favoured occupations and skills
Comarenza – large island in the western Inner Sea
The Company – self-styling used by Kiergard Slorn's mercenary band
The Confederacy – the Confederate Nations and Territories of Pelledac. Powerful state in the north-east of Mehan'Gir
Corvak – ancient state in Mehan'Gir, famed for its Dams, Lakes and Cities
Crow – one of the Nine Clans, the clan of Thieves

Dach – familiar name of Pireon's older brother, Dachaeron, slightly younger twin to Dasha
Prince Dalleric – third and youngest son of the Emperor Athendor. After an abortive attempt to seize power, he fled the Court and operated as a mercenary using the name Kiergard Slorn
Dark Elves – the Madarinn
Darkfall – northernmost town in the Three Lands, where the mid-winter Festival of the Crown is held
Dasha – familiar name of Pireon's older sister, Adastana, slightly older twin to Dach
Davata Lodge – Kiergard Slorn's property on Calinnia
The Dead God – the major deity in Corvak's Pantheon of Gods and across the Three Lands
Death Squads – Confederacy assassination units
Deon – oldest child of Amphet and Ilada
Dimir – one of the Twelve Gods of Corvak, the God of Death and the Land Beyond
Dog – one of the Nine Clans, the clan of Fighters
Dragon Lords – creatures of legend, possibly one of the Four Races
Dragon Sea – sea between Mehan'Gir and Qassiq'Gir, bounded by the Inner Sea on the west and the Ashadic Sea on the north-east
Durac – the Blind God of Hope. Worshipped by the Brothers of Duraxi

Eagle – one of the Nine Clans, the clan of Priests and Healers
Eastholm – port on the Inner Sea, east of the White Mountains
King Edrinn – Vy'Rhienn's father, killed during the fall of Ruthin
Ehrenmouth – small port on the Inner Sea
Elagion – one of the Twenty-Two Floating Cities of Corvak: home of the Mother Temple, the Oracle and the Seminary Complex
Kai Elidar – name by which Lanvik is addressed by Doctor Gossine and Kai Arlech
Elisha of Giren Pass – one of Redwolf's Madarinn officers, who formed an instant mutual attraction with Kiergard Slorn
Elves – the Terevarna and Madarinn, two of the Four Races
The Emerald Crown – one of the Four Trophies of the Dead God, taken by Kiergard Slorn from Darkfall
Emindur – the Imperial Capital
The Empire – the most powerful state in Mehan'Gir, controlling most of the land west of the White Mountains
Enixis – most southerly of Corvak's Floating Cities, in Lake Visander
Ephander – Pireon's paternal grandfather, former head of the Kiritas family
Prince Eriskant – third and youngest brother of the Emperor Athendor, uncle to Silvendor and Dalleric. Killed by Foxblade in Haadar
Ethryk – Madarinn member of Kiergard Slorn's Company

Floating Cities – Corvak has twenty-two Floating Cities
Four Lakes – giant lakes in Corvak, created by a series of dams across the Great River
Four Trophies – the Emerald Crown, the Ruby Hand, the Glass Sword and another: according to legend, they possess magical properties
Foxblade – Atterlie's Chapter Name
Free Ports – several independent and unregulated ports along the Illian Shore
Fugitive – popular board game

Garran – Terevarna Member of Kiergard Slorn's Company. Dog clan
The Glass Sword – one of the Four Trophies of the Dead God
The Great Families – eighteen families in Corvak, whose heads form one of the three ruling Councils
The Great River – largest river in Mehan'Gir: its basin forms the Steppes, and it flows into the Inner Sea at the Delta in Corvak

Haadar – small port on the Human Shore where Prince Eriskant was killed
Halldyn – Kiergard Slorn's aged Terevarna retainer at Davata Lodge
Harruth Atravon – legendary Messenger of the Four Races and the Gods, who guards the souls of the Vampire Brood
Heklash of the Storms – "Mad Heklash", one of the Twelve Gods of Corvak

Hengerad – the royal house of Ruthin
Lord Navin Hesketh – ally and lieutenant of Prince Silvendor
Hierarch – highest rank of the Priesthood of Corvak, currently Ykerios
Hindera – largest of the three moons
Humans – probably one of the Four Races

Ialyssa – Pireon's aunt, daughter of his father's aunt Tamina
Iera – student at the Oracle School on Elagion
Ilada – pairbond of Pireon's uncle Amphet
Inner Sea – sea between Mehan'Gir and Qassiq'Gir, bounded by the Isthmus on the west and the Dragon Sea on the east
Jetta Ir Shann – high-ranking Confederacy official, responsible for Internal Security
The Iron Gate – gate in Ruthin across the only pass through the White Mountains open all year
The Isthmus – narrow stretch of land linking Mehan'Gir and Qassiq'Gir

Ja'Orr – one of the Twelve Gods of Corvak, the Healer of Bodies

Karithia – north-eastern peninsula and most recent State of the Confederacy
Kayoden – island in Corvak, home of Pireon's family's estate
The Keep – the original defensible building of Ravensgill's Royal Palace
Kiritas – one of Corvak's Great Families, to which Pireon belongs
Cold Korridan – one of the twelve Gods of Corvak
Kylos Fern – mountainous location where mages are trained

Land of Mists – Ceran'Don, the Eastern Continent
Lanvik (1) – capital and main town of Urthgard
Lanvik (2) – name given by Kiergard Slorn's Company to the mage they rescued
Lavana – Pireon's mother, pairbond of Timaerion, known as Vana
Light Elves – the Terevarna
Linnander – state in the Western Steppes, northwest of Cerinium
Lisamel – Terevarna member of the Company. Sparrow clan

Madarinn – the Dark Elves
Magda – Terevarna member of Kiergard Slorn's Company, and youngest. Crow clan
Magda's Choice – a small ketch, formerly used by Kiergard Slorn's Company
Mages – users of magecraft, invariably human, known by their staff and shaved head
Mehan'Gir – the Northern Continent
Menska – Terevarna member of Kiergard Slorn's Company, Eagle clan
Prince Mironyx – Atterlie's younger brother, known as Miko
Mossdale – closest settlement to the Imperial Compound in the Arvedan Hills

Mountain Bear – One of the Nine Clans, the clan of Manual Labourers

Neophyte – any member of the Priesthood below the rank of Junior Priest
Night Princess – three-masted frigate, and pirate ship of Captain Redwolf
Nisia – small port on the island of Stoli

The Oracle – shares the island of Elagion with the Seminary and the Mother Temple

The Pantheon – the Twelve Gods of Corvak
Pelledac – capital of the Confederacy, on the Kyllian Firth
Perina – state in the northern Steppes, bordering the Confederacy
Phoenix – one of the Nine Clans, the clan of Artisans
Piastamo – part-time cook at Davata Lodge
Pireon of Kiritas – Priest-Acolyte studying at the Seminary on Elagion
Port Evendar – main Imperial port on the Inner Sea
The Psirogant – most senior figure in the Oracle on Elagion

Qassiq'Gir – the Southern Continent
Quinara – one of the Twelve Gods of Corvak. The Goddess or Keeper of the Old Knowledge
Quiron – Timo's brother and, after his death, head of the Kiritas family

Ravensgill – capital of Ruthin, east of the Iron Gate
Captain Redwolf – identity used by General Aravan, operating as a pirate
The House of Roeven – branch of the Imperial Family to which Vy'Rhienn's mother Arenima belonged
The Ruby Hand – one of the Four Trophies of the Dead God, stolen by Kiergard Slorn from the Confederacy
Ruthin – small Duchy, formerly a Kingdom, that controls the Iron Gate

Scarthann – home base of the Imperial Western Fleet, on West Durrant
The Seminary – the religious school of Mother Church, on Elagion
Lord Sephraim – one of the Twelve Gods of Corvak, the God of Journeys, Madarinn and Soldiers. Also known as the prince that walks the land and kills
Sha'hann, the Voice – one of the twelve Gods of Corvak, the blind goddess of prophecy and the future
Shamura – large city in south-east Mehan'Gir, once capital of a maritime empire
Shark – one of the Nine Clans, the clan of Instructors, Politicians and Administrators
Shuramak – smallest and fastest of the three moons

Crown Prince Silvendor – eldest son of Emperor Athendor the Eighth
The Sisters of the Silent Blade – one of the six Chapters of the Assassin's Guild. Atterlie's Chapter
Sivunder – peninsula of Qassiq'Gir, between the Inner Sea and the Dragon Sea
Kiergard Slorn – identity used by Dalleric, as leader of a Company of mercenaries
Sparrow – one of the Nine Clans, the clan of Artists, Performers and Prostitutes
Armagon Stengiss – leader of the Confederacy's most feared Death Squad
The Steppes – the fertile and largely flat basin of the Great River
Stoli – small island in the Inner Sea close to Calinnia
Duke Struving – Imperial aristocrat who assumed the throne of Ruthin

Nemendir Tarq – previously Base Commander at An'Holt
Terevarna – the Light Elves
Thawn – Terevarna member of Kiergard Slorn's company. Dog clan
Thieving Priest – a large ketch, recently acquired by Kiergard Slorn's Company
Timaerion – Pireon's father, former head of the Kiritas family
Timo – familiar name of Timaerion, Pireon's father
Tohros – one of the Twelve Gods of Corvak, the Healer of Souls
Tremano – Terevarna member of Kiergard Slorn's Company, Sparrow clan
Tyrell – Terevarna member of Kiergard Slorn's company. Dog clan. Garran's cousin

Uri – father of Amphet and older brother of Uthraiche
Uthraiche – Pireon's intimidating Great Aunt

Vallierta – large city on the western side of Carissola
Vampire Brood – creatures of legend, possibly one of the Four Races
Vana – familiar name of Lavana, Pireon's mother
Vander – the sacrificial Tribute from Arrento, rescued and now a member of Kiergard Slorn's Company
Vinderich – elder son of Duke Struving of Ruthin
Els Vorrigan – Terevarna member of Kiergard Slorn's Company, Wolf clan
Vrosko Din Havell – Terevarna member of Kiergard Slorn's Company, Eagle clan
Princess Vy'Rhienn – younger daughter of King Edrinn of Ruthin. She fled Ravensgill during the coup, aged eight and joined the Guild of Assassins under the name Atterlie

West Durrant – large island at the southern end of the Durrandir Spine. Home to the naval base of Scarthann

The White Mountains – highest range of mountains in Mehan'Gir, running roughly north/south

Wolf – one of the Nine Clans, the clan of Merchants and Traders

Ykerios – current Hierarch of Corvak

Printed in Great Britain
by Amazon